Into Egypt: Enemies

Angelique Conger

SOUTHWEST OF ZION

To those who struggle against enemies
within and without.

Contents

Ludim

Egyptus sat in her newly built home of stone and wood copying the Book of Commandments for the last time until another couple married. Every family in Egypt had received a copy except Animim and Gilit. A sadness filled her knowing her friend refused to learn to read, and in that refusal, refused to receive a copy of the sacred book coming from their first parent, Adam.

Egyptus had promised Animim the last book, if he would help her get the needed papyrus. In the three years since Gilit had rebuffed her offer of a copy of the book for her family, he had quietly brought papyrus to her each month while it grew tall. His help had eased Egyptus's burden. She could focus on making the papyrus pages and copying the words of the book onto them. She worked now to finish his book, ignoring the cramp growing in her back from sitting at her table for so long.

Someone blew the shell from the top of the wall. The unexpected, loud warning jarred and startled her, causing her to drop her pen on the page. She hurriedly snatched it up, set the pen to the side, and stared at the nearly completed page. A blob of ink stained it.

The sound sent a strand of fear through her. An enemy approached. No stranger had come to trade since they settled in Egypt, only men seeking to take what did not belong to them. The call beckoned her to her fighting place near the wall.

I will have to fix that later. So close to the end ...

She sighed and shoved her chair back, hurried to the door, and grabbed her staff before trotting out to join her assigned group to help push back the invaders. She joined Cira and Chayim, who led the group responsible to guard the back wall farthest from the gate.

When Pharoah first assigned them this position, Levi had complained. "How can we do our part to protect Egypt if we are assigned to the back wall of the village?"

"We cannot expect all the invaders to come through the gates," Pharoah had said. "Some will climb the wall or try to set it on fire. We need groups to protect all our walls, not just the front wall and gate."

In the first attack, the enemy leader had sent men to scale the back wall, thinking to sneak in and capture women. Since then, Levi no longer complained about the group's assignment.

Egyptus glanced up into a cloudless blue sky. Rain would help keep the enemies away. None tried to scale their walls in the rain and the mud would slow their steps to and from the walls.

Chayim, Levi, and five other men climbed the steps to the walkway with spears and bows, watching for invaders. Younger boys and girls had gathered stones and placed them in baskets along the walkway. They had then pulled them up to the walkway with ropes and spaced them out evenly, ready to drop the rocks onto any enemy's head who tried to climb up the wall.

Now they waited, listening to the shouts of attacking men outside the walls of their village.

What do the attackers think they will get from an attack? Gold or silver? Not from us. We have none. Food? Perhaps. Women? None they want. We are too independent.

Egyptus glanced at the other women waiting with her. None of these women would cheerfully go with attacking men. They would fight them, and if taken, would fight them until they escaped. She shook her head.

Silly men to attack us. Silly to think they could take women from Egypt.

Egyptus had brought her family and friends to this area before Jehovah had changed the languages of all who still lived in Shinar, forcing them to separate. She clearly remembered the dream visions of that time, watching her brothers shouting at her mama and papa. It had frightened her, not knowing if they were dreams or visions until a group of strange men trekked through their lands three years earlier.

Corom had ridden off alone to greet them and invite members of their family not seen for years to join them in the village. He had returned with a knife in his arm, alive only because his horse had reared as the leader of the small group threw the poisoned knife. That event had compelled Egyptus to share her dream visions with the others in her village.

Over the past three years, sightings of wandering groups increased, as did the attacks on Egypt's walls. These groups grew larger each time they attacked. No one thought of inviting wandering groups inside the walls of the village anymore. Not after that first attack on Corom.

The noise of shouting men outside the wall lessened. Levi poked his head over the top of the wall to see why.

"They think they can climb the wall," he growled softly. "They have ropes."

"They think they will succeed in the attack here at the back when they cannot in the front?" Chayim responded in quiet contempt. "We will show them Egypt is not an easy target for them."

Egyptus glanced at the women who stood with staffs in their hands. "Are you ready?"

Determination filled the women's faces as they nodded in silent agreement.

They gazed at the back wall and the walkway near the top. A heavy hemp rope, knotted at one end, bumped against the top of the wall. Levi stepped forward and pushed the rope away from the wall.

"Argh!" a voice cried from the other side of the wall.

Soft complaining sounds, then the knotted end of another heavy rope flew over the wall and caught between the lengthwise logs.

"Be prepared," Egyptus whispered. "They will climb that rope soon."

"Not if I can pull it from between these logs," Chayim cried as he pushed on the knot. Levi joined him, but they could not remove it.

Squeaking and soft thumps on the wall warned them that someone was climbing the rope. Levi chose a good-sized rock from the basket near his feet. He leaned over the wall and dropped the rock.

A man yelped.

"He did not fall," Levi growled, leaning out to see.

Chayim and the other men took rocks from the basket and took turns dropping them on the climbers. They heard attackers cry out as they were hit and fell.

But more ropes flew over the top of the wall, more than the men could push away. Levi and his men continued to drop rocks on the attackers' heads, but that did not deter them. The tops of enemy heads appeared over the top.

"They come," Cira whispered.

Holding the staff loosely in her hands, Egyptus'whipped it up to the ready position, as did the other women's staffs, as they waited for the attackers. She hoped the men of her fighting group could stop them on the walkway. However, in past attacks, they had learned it did not happen often enough. Attackers pushed past them and leapt to the ground, the anger changing to a leering greed when they saw the women waiting for them.

"Remember to focus," Egyptus muttered.

Heads nodded as the women kept their focus on the wall. They had learned from previous attacks to pay attention to different sections after the strange men, now enemies, leapt into the village while other men and women focused on a battle in the center. One day an attacker had caught Rebecca and tried to drag her through the village. Before he could take her far, Kib had run forward and smashed the hilt of his sword on the back of the attacker's head.

Egyptus swept her glance across the group of women, each woman focused on the wall. She turned her gaze upward to the top. The Egyptian men wrestled with the attackers, using swords against the intruders' knives and swords. Egyptus feared there would be injuries among their group this time.

Without thinking, Egyptus shouted, "Be careful."

Her men turned toward her, taking their eyes off the intruders for a short breath. An attacker pushed away from Shim and leapt toward her and the other women.

Egyptus held her staff ready as he jumped toward her. He flexed his knees as he dropped and came to a stand, staring at her and shouting undecipherable words. He sneered as recognition filled his eyes.

"Ludim?" she gasped.

The attacker growled and charged toward her, a huge, black knife with jagged edges filled his hand.

Egyptus did not hesitate. She brought her staff up and hit his hands, trying to knock away the knife. He clung to it. She hit him on the side of the head. The other women would continue to watch for others to bound off the walkway as they tried capture a woman, but she kept her focus on Ludim.

He stretched out, grabbing for her staff. She spun it around, dropped it low, then whirled around, hitting him below his knees.

Ludim shouted and wobbled, but soon regained his balance. He snarled at Egyptus and lunged toward her. She stepped aside as she had practiced many times while sparring with other women. He missed and charged past her.

She turned in time to catch him on the side with her staff as he charged toward her once more with a roar. She yanked her staff back and popped him forcefully on the top of his head.

Ludim slumped to the ground, his knife finally falling from his fist.

Egyptus glanced around to see if other attackers had leapt from the walkway or toward the other women. Breathing heavily from her efforts, she knew she would help defend the others until the last attacker had fallen. Another man lay on the ground, quietly moaning. Ludim lay unmoving.

Egyptus stood guard with the other women while the men continued to battle their attackers on the walkway. No more men dropped over the edge.

Levi pushed his attacker backwards over the wall. The attacker's shout echoed as he fell. He then turned to help Chayim fight another enemy. Together, they tipped him over the edge of the wall. The men fought against three more attackers, pushing one as a prisoner to the walkway, tipping another over the wall, and backing the last off the walkway.

With their staffs ready, the women waited to take on any who managed to break free. One man fell backward and hit his head hard on the ground. He lifted his head once, then dropped it back to the ground, moaning.

Jason grabbed woven papyrus ropes and tied the arms of the man who lay on the walkway behind his back. Shim and Chayim grabbed the man by the arms and pulled him to his feet. They pushed him down the stairs and set him with the three men Egyptus and her women guarded.

"That man looks familiar," Chayim said, pointing toward Ludim. "He is dirtier than I remember. His beard and hair are long and shaggy and he looks unloved. Still, he looks like someone I once knew."

"He should look familiar. He is my nephew, Ludim. His wife, Niva, led the attack on me that forced me to leave Shinar." Egyptus nudged Ludim with the toe of her shoe. "I saw him beat Niva almost to death in my dreams. I would not want to find myself alone with him without my staff. It was difficult to overcome him."

"The Ludim I remember was a kind man. He would bring me fresh strawberries," Cira said. "This man is not that friendly man."

"No. He is angry," Egyptus said. "Could you comprehend any words these men spoke?"

"It was all garbled," Levi said from the walkway. He leaned over the wall. "Our attackers are gone except for the three we dumped over the wall. They do not look like they survived."

Egyptus sighed. She hated hurting these men, even as they were attacking her. A death of one or more would be distressing.

"We will need to repent," she muttered.

"Repent?" Devora squeaked. "They attacked us!"

"But we may have taken some of their lives," Egyptus said with a shiver.

We would not have taken their lives if they had left us alone," Chayim growled.

"They brought it on themselves," Cira pouted.

"Perhaps they did, but I do not want to have their lives darkening my soul," Egyptus said.

Ludim stirred at her feet, struggling with the bindings that tied his hands behind his back. The sounds that came from him sounded like curses, though she could not comprehend his words.

She bumped him on the head with her staff and hissed at him. "Shh. Be quiet."

"What will we do with these men?" Levi asked.

"How did they get so many together to attack us?" Chayim asked. "I thought they could not speak to each other."

The hot fragrance of anger still filled the air.

Egyptus shrugged and shook her head, not knowing how it happened. She gazed around, hoping Pharoah would soon be around to see how those who fought far away from the gate had fared. The sounds of fighting there had dropped to almost nothing.

"Where is Pharoah?" Rebecca asked. "He needs to do something with these men."

Egyptus bent to check the ties of a man who moaned next to Ludim. He rolled from his face to his back and shoved his fist upward, trying to punch her. She flinched away from it.

"Oh, no, I will not allow that," Alma growled, slapping her staff against the man's fist.

Devora's staff followed, hitting him in the head. "He should not have done that."

Timor bent to bang the attacker's head with the hilt of his sword.

"No need," Egyptus said, reaching out to stop the sword's movement. Her heart pounded loud enough she wondered if the attacker could hear it. "Devora took care of him. While you are there, will you bind his hands?"

Timor flipped the attacker back onto his face and tied his hands tight enough he would not escape again.

"Esrom," Timor called, "go see if Pharoah is free. We have four prisoners."

Esrom shoved his sword into its sheath and trotted down the lane toward the front gate.

"He fought well," Timor said, nodding toward Esrom's retreating figure. "I did not expect him to do so well. He stopped an attacker before he could attack me."

Egyptus sighed. These attacks on her village frustrated her. *If these men would try to communicate with us, we could help them. We have enough to share — a little to share. They want to take what we have worked hard to gather and preserve.*

"Mama?" Timor asked, touching Egyptus's shoulder.

Egyptus jerked out of her thoughts. "What?"

"I asked about him." Timor pointed at Ludim. "Is that not our cousin?"

Egyptus nodded. "It is. That is Ludim. He has changed." His anger and hatred shocked her. Before she could say more, Pharoah strode toward them.

"Esrom says you have some prisoners," he said.

Timor jerked a thumb at the four men lying on the ground. "The women captured three. We captured this one," he pointed to the man near Ludim. "We tossed three more over the wall. This was a bigger group than we usually fight."

"Is that Ludim?" Pharoah asked, pointing at him. His frown showed his disgust at the changes in him.

"Yes," Egyptus said. "Were there as many to battle on your side of the village?"

Pharoah sighed. "Yes. And more. How did they gather this many men together to fight against us? I thought they could not speak to each other?"

He stepped over to Ludim and bent to pull him up from the ground. Timor grabbed Ludim by the other shoulder and helped lift him up.

"Why are you here?" Pharoah growled.

Ludim attempted to open a swollen eye. "Mmm?"

"What are you doing here?" Pharoah asked once more.

Ludim moved his head back and forth. He made a sound, but Egyptus could not comprehend the words.

"How did they gather so many together? We must have fought off twenty or twenty-five men. I did not think they could get together if they could not comprehend each other." Pharoah nodded toward the gathering place near the gate. "We should take these to join their friends."

"Friends?" Levi asked.

"Yes. We captured three more. The others ran away. Can you keep the others here until we get back?" Pharoah nodded at the other men lying on the ground.

"We captured them," Cira said. "We can keep them here until you return."

Pharoah and Timor dragged Ludim away. Levi and Chayim pulled up another prisoner, dragging him between them walking behind Pharoah.

The women stood around the last two captured and semi-conscious men with their staffs ready to hit them if they tried to escape.

Timor and Pharoah returned with more men to drag away the men the women had captured. Chayim grabbed the last prisoner by the elbow, lifting him up with Jakob's help. They dragged each enemy between two men down the stairs, grunting and groaning as they bounced down each step, and down the path. Egyptus and the other women followed behind.

Blindfolds

At the gathering place near the gate, Egyptus saw more men bound as her fighting group had bound their prisoners. Ludim sat with his head bowed to his knees. Hateful sounding words poured from his mouth.

"What is he saying?" Xenia asked, pointing to Ludim.

Egyptus shrugged. "His words hold no meaning for me, but by the tone of his voice, I believe he is angry we captured him."

Ludim lifted his head and stared at her. Venom greater than before caused his face to twist. His voice lifted. He expelled words sounding like curses. He stopped, coughed, and spat in Egyptus's direction.

Pharoah strode through the knot of men and slammed his fist into Ludim's face, knocking him on his side. "You will not spit at my mama, nor will you speak like that to her," he thundered.

"I believe Ludim is angry with me. But I did not cause any of his troubles," Egyptus said.

"No," Isa said, moving to stand beside her. "But in his mind you have caused everything that happened to him."

Egyptus turned to her friend. "Can you make sense of his words?"

Isa shook her head. "Not the words, but the tone and the vicious stare. He thinks you caused him to be here."

Egyptus barked a short laugh. "Me? I left the plains of Shinar because his wife tried to kill me. He tried to kill her. How could I cause his problems?"

"You did not," Isa said. "What does it matter? In his mind, you are the cause."

Egyptus ducked her head. *I do not know why he would blame me.* "I did nothing to him or to Niva. I ..."

Isa put an arm around her. "It is his problem, not yours."

Egyptus lifted her head and stared at Ludim laying on the ground. Even though his lip bled into the dirt, he growled his unrecognizable curse words, known by their venom. He turned his head and stared at her.

"Egyptus," he spat.

"Ludim," she responded.

A string of incomprehensible vulgar sounds escaped his lips before Pharoah lifted his fist.

"Ludim! Enough."

Ludim stopped babbling and turned his stare toward Pharoah. He sneered and spoke another string of venom-filled words.

"What will you do with them?" Arvad asked.

Pharoah nodded toward a space away from the prisoners. "We will discuss this away from here. Jakob, Chayim, Levi, stay here and guard these men. We will share our discussion later."

The three men nodded and pulled their swords from their sheaths, allowing the vibrations to ring the swords.

Egyptus looked at the women around her. Cira nodded to Marji, Ester, and Lexa. "We will join the men and help guard the prisoners."

The women lifted their staffs.

"They will not try to escape," Marji said.

Egyptus followed Pharoah and the other Egyptians away from their prisoners to discuss what to do without being overheard, and still be nearby in case of trouble.

"What will we do?" Akish asked. "If we release them, they will return. If we kill them, we will be murderers. I do not want to be a murderer, but I do not want these men to return and attack us."

"Perhaps they will see that we are stronger than them and leave," Meyer suggested.

"We can feed them and send them away," Gilit said.

"They will return for more, like the animals they —" Shiblom growled.

"How do we send them away and ensure they do not return?" Isa cut him off.

The community members argued about the problem, a few wanting to release them, while a few others were willing to find a different solution.

"Ludim will return now he knows you are here, Egyptus," Isa said, "as he blames you for his problems. If we do not take his life or do something to keep him far away, he will return."

Egyptus bit her lower lip and bent her head. *There must be a better solution. What can we do to teach them to stay far from us?*

"We must pray about this," Pharoah said. "I do not care if those men see us pray."

They all knelt in the damp dirt and lifted their hands in prayer. Pharoah led the prayer, begging Jehovah to help them resolve the problem in a way He would approve. "We do not desire to take their lives," he prayed, "but we need them to leave and never return. What can we do?"

When they finished praying, they knelt in the dirt a long time, listening to the answer that filled their hearts.

Egyptus's heart warmed. She knew they would have an answer. She waited for Pharoah and the other men to receive their answer as well.

"I know," Shiblom said quietly. "We can blindfold them and take them far from our village. We can build a fire to keep the wild animals away and leave them with enough food for two days. We will warn them ..."

"They will return," Gilit said in a flat voice.

"No, Gilit," Animim said. "I, too, received this answer. The wild animals will warn them to stay far away."

"For how long?" Alma asked.

"Wild animals?" Gilit squeaked.

"I do not know how," Pharoah said. "But Jehovah will protect us with wild animals."

Egyptus set her hand on her heart, accepting the rightness of the answer. "When do we take them away?"

"Now," Pharoah said. "Xenia, take some other women with you to gather a basket of food for them. Mama, can you find blindfolds for them?"

Xenia nodded, and Bilhah and Dora left with her. Egyptus turned and walked toward her home.

"Emer, go hook the donkeys to the wagon," Pharoah said.

Egyptus heard him giving other men instructions as she moved farther away and could no longer hear his voice clearly. Inside her home, she entered her workspace, searching for cloths she could use for blindfolds.

Looking around her home, she saw strips of soaked papyrus. She picked one up and wrapped it around her face.

Sticky, but it will keep the light out. And it will not entice wild animals.

She searched through the lengths of papyrus and found five long enough to wrap around the prisoners' heads.

It is not nice, but it will serve Ludim right. He should not threaten me. She sighed.

Is this the solution? He does not deserve the sticky on his face, and I need the papyrus to copy the Book of Commandments.

She dug through a bag filled with scraps of fabric left from making clothing. She found a length from the fabric left over from Rebecca's marriage.

This is nicer than the papyrus. I do not need to make Ludim angrier with me, and I need the papyrus for other things.

She returned the papyrus to the container, then tore the length of fabric into five strips. She carried them to the village gathering place and the prisoners. Xenia and her daughters joined her as she passed by.

"Did you find blindfolds?" Dora asked.

Egyptus held up the lengths of fabric from Rebecca's dress. "These are softer than the papyrus I considered."

"That would be sticky!" Bilhah gasped. "But they would deserve it."

"I do not need Ludim to have reason to be angrier with me. He has enough anger as it is. Did you get food?"

"We got enough for two days from the storehouses. It is not visible from the gate, so they will not know where to look for more if they return," Xenia said.

Egyptus nodded. "Good. I hope they never return. I hope this causes the wanderers to share their plight with others and decide we are not an easy target for them to attack."

"How can they if they do not speak the same language?" Bilhah asked.

"How did they get thirty men together to attack today?" Egyptus countered with a shrug.

The wagon waited near the prisoners, waiting for them to be loaded. Egyptus glanced up at the sun, surprised to see it had just reached its zenith. The men who took the prisoners would have time to get them far away and still return before night.

"Here is the food," Xenia said, setting the basket under the seat of the wagon.

"Here are strips of fabric to use as blindfolds," Egyptus said, holding up the scraps of fabric.

"Is that from my —" Rebecca asked.

"Yes, but these men need not know," Egyptus said, stopping her question mid-sentence.

Rebecca glanced toward the prisoners. "They do not comprehend our words."

"No need to take a chance on that," Egyptus said. "I thought of bringing papyrus instead, but I have a better use for it."

"And it would stick to their faces," Animim said with a little chortle.

"If these men ever return, they will get papyrus for blindfolds," Egyptus declared.

She stepped toward the prisoners, but Arvad stopped her. "You do not need to have their filth brush onto you, Mama Egyptus. I will blindfold them." He took the strips of cloth from her and gently pushed her away.

Moans and shouting erupted from the prisoners as Arvad tied blindfolds tightly around their eyes. The acrid smell of fear and lost body water filled the air. Ludim's curses continued.

"Do not return," Pharoah said to each man as he and Shiblom lifted them onto the wagon. Jakob and Meyer moved each man to a place in the wagon away from the others.

"Will they know what you are saying?" Isa asked.

"Even if they do not comprehend my words, they need to hear them," Pharoah said.

Esrom sat in the driver's seat. After loading the prisoners, Jakob, Myer, Levi, Chayim, and Jason sat between the prisoners so they could not communicate or fight back.

"Take them to the edge of the valley and build a fire with the wood in the wagon," Pharoah said. "Leave them blindfolded. They can remove the blindfolds after you are gone. If wild animals prowl close to them before they remove the blindfolds, good."

"Got it," Esrom said. "Take them out to the edge, build a fire, and leave them with the food."

"Then hurry home as fast as your donkeys can travel," Cira said. "I need you home."

Chayim jumped from the wagon to kiss Cira and hug their little son. He patted her stomach where a new child waited for its birth. "We will be back before dark."

"Please do," Cira said as he climbed back into the wagon. Esrom flicked the reins across the donkeys' rumps and they slowly rumbled past the gates. Moren and Animim closed the gates behind the wagon.

Pym climbed to the top of the walkway. "It is my turn to watch. I will watch them as far as I can see them while I watch for other attackers."

"You think there will be more attackers?" Bilhah asked her husband, rubbing her swollen stomach. She, Cira, and Rebecca would give birth within a month of each other.

"Stranger things have happened," Pym said.

"I hope not tonight," Bilhah murmured and waved to Pym.

"I pray Jehovah protects us from others who believe we have something to take because we built walls," Egyptus said. "Our walls protected us from wild animals originally. Now they must also protect us from wild men."

A lion roared outside the wall. "See," she said.

She walked with Bilhah to her home before returning to her own little house. The pages of papyrus lay on her table, waiting for her to return and complete the last copy of the Book of Commandments.

She sighed as she saw the blob of ink on the page.

Only three pages to write, and this one has ink spoiling it in the center. It would be nice if attacking men would wait until I finish this.

Egyptus picked up her stone scraper and gently scraped away the ink blob that spoiled the page.

I can fix this, but I cannot fix Ludim's problems. I hope he stays far away from Egypt.

She scraped away most of the ink, then looked back at her writing, finding her place. She lifted her pen from the pot she used to hold her pens, dipped it in the small pot of ink, brushed the tip against the edge so it would not drip, and then wrote the next word.

It would surprise Animim when she gave him a copy of the book. She had mentioned to him when she began copying it onto this scroll for him, but he never asked when it would be completed. He had only shaken his head, tossing it toward Gilit, who continued to have no use for the sacred book.

What would happen to Animim when Gilit finally pushed her nasty attitude too far? Others might insist she leave Egypt if she did not contain her displeasure.

Since the day three years ago, when they had warned all the women to stop wasting their precious food, it no longer had dwindled at an unseemly rate. And no one had reported seeing a woman giving large cuts of meat to her dog. Perhaps Gilit had taken the warning to heart and would finally do her part.

Egyptus snorted to herself. "Gilit sees herself as better than any of the rest of us. Why would she do her part? She often does only what is required to maintain her status as a member of the village."

Shaking her head, Egyptus focused on the words she wrote, reminded by them of her need to have charity and love for all.

Even Gilit.

Egyptus allowed her thoughts to roam as she wrote. Three women would have children soon: Rebecca, Cira, and Bilhah. More children would join their ever-growing family and the community of Egypt. They would need to extend the walls before long. More young people paired off, desiring the marriage rite. She would need to create gifts for the babies and the young couples.

She expelled her breath. More young couples meant a need for more copies of the Book of Commandments. The task would never end.

Spans later, Egyptus heard the shout of men at the gate. She wrote the last word in the Book of Commandments for Animim and carefully set her pen in the jar with the others. She capped her ink jar, then gently sprinkled sand across the words on the papyrus.

Only then did she push her chair back and move toward the door, wondering how the prisoners had reacted to the resolution Pharoah and the others had devised to avoid killing them.

Egyptus reached the gathering place as Chayim leapt from the wagon seat and grabbed Cira, whirling her around. "We are home before dark," he cried, "and I doubt those men will bother us again."

"Nor for a while at least," Esrom said, less cheerfully than Chayim.

"Ludim never stopped cursing us," Meyer said, shaking his head. "Even as he slept, curses escaped his lips. I feel sorry for a man who finds no joy in life."

Isa stepped next to Egyptus. "He brought it on himself," she whispered.

"I know," Egyptus murmured back. "But I still cannot comprehend such hatred."

Pharoah stood at the side of the wagon as the men climbed from it. "How did it go? Did you leave them able to escape?"

"We built a fire to keep wild animals away, set them around it, and left the basket of food, as you ordered," Jakob said. He stepped to the donkeys, preparing to lead them to the barn and the meal they had earned. His wife, Chana, joined him. "Many of them were sleepy from the long ride. We left the blindfolds on them. It will take them longer to free themselves."

"I am certain at least one of them had his ties loosened before we left," Jason said. "He sat quietly working the ties loose when he thought no one watched." He hugged his new wife, Devora. "But I watched him."

"As did I," Levi added. "If he had worked his hands free, we would have tied them again. But he did not free them before we set him on the ground beside the fire." He pulled Lexa into an embrace. The community would soon celebrate their marriage rite.

"He will be first to enjoy the food," Jason said, running his fingers through Devora's long, dark hair. "I wonder if he will set his companions free."

"That is his problem, and those of his companions," Meyer said. His arms encircled Ada's waist. "Men like that —"

"Soon become close friends. He will help his friends," Jakob said. "As for Ludim, I do not know how anyone could befriend a man as angry as him. Ho!" he called to the donkeys, starting them toward the barn. "Even donkeys are better friends."

The lead donkey brayed.

"You are a good friend," Chana said, petting the animal's neck. "Jakob knows you are better than that weasel, Ludim."

"Even a weasel is better than Ludim," Isa murmured.

Egyptus chuckled softly. "Even weasels? Poor Ludim."

"Do you think those men will be safe from wild animals until they free themselves from the ties?" Pharoah asked.

"We saw hyenas creeping close to them, but the fire will keep them away," Meyer said. "They should be safe until the fire burns down."

"Was there more wood for them to add to their fire?" Xenia asked.

"Not close. If they want more wood, they will have to gather it for themselves," Chayim said. "We provided a ride, fire, and food. That is more than they would do for us."

Jason and Levi nodded in agreement.

"That Ludim would rather kill us than help us," Levi said. "He will return, even with the cats surrounding the village."

"Cats?" Egyptus asked.

"Yes. Cats," Jason said. "Big cats. Lions, tigers, and leopards surround our walls. I feared we would have to battle the cats to enter, but they moved aside for us to reach the gate. I did not expect them to do that."

"I watched from the wall," Pym said. "After the men left, big cats slowly left the high grasses and moved toward Egypt. Each family of cats claimed a space, then laid down. I waited to see what they would do when our men returned. Usually, they like donkeys as easy food, but today they moved aside, making way for our men to return."

"Will they allow our enemies to move past them so easily?" Xenia asked.

Pym shrugged. "We will have to watch and see."

"Are we imprisoned inside our own walls?" Gilit asked, clutching her arms around her chest.

"Perhaps," Pym said. "I would not want to go out among those big cats today. Jehovah sent them to watch over us, but I would not give them reason to forget."

"It is good we have food and water inside," Animim said, embracing Gilit. "Pharoah's wisdom shows yet again as we have the well he directed us to dig."

"And sent an early flood with animals for us to harvest. No men will want to attack us while the cats surround our walls," Bilhah said. "Will you still stand watch?"

"My turn ended," Pym said.

"And it is now my turn," Shez said, setting a foot on the bottom stair to the walkway. "I suspect I will have an easy watch."

"You can watch the cats sleep," Angetta said.

"Or watch them hunt," Shez said.

"Do not fall asleep while watching the cats," Pharoah said as Shez bounced up the stairs.

"I would not do that," Shez called from the top. "You can trust me. Besides, I want to see what the cats will do."

"Do you really think Jehovah sent them?" Hibah asked.

"We prayed for protection," Pharoah said. "We need relief from the attacks of our enemy. Those big cats will keep our enemies away and allow us to rest. We should give thanks to Jehovah."

Jakob and Chana returned as the villagers knelt where they stood, in the dirt and greenery of the village square, to join Pharoah in giving thanks to Jehovah for sending wild animals to protect them.

"And bless those men who would attack us. Help them find other ways to meet their needs. Help them find a home and family so they will no longer want to take ours from us," Pharoah said before he ended his prayer.

Egyptus repeated the words with a silent 'amen'. If these men and others found a home and family, they would no longer desire to steal from Egypt's small community.

Big Cats

Men watched for enemies from the walkway during the next days in rain and shine. During the day, women and children joined the men on the walkway, staring out between the wall and the river and into the fields and the tall grass surrounding the village. In those spaces, families of lions, tigers and leopards lazed. Sometimes the lionesses roused themselves from the earth to stalk animals that stopped at the Black River for a drink. Tigers and leopards took turns hunting.

Egyptus looked toward the river with Ami and Rivka early one morning. The acrid scent of all the big cats filled the air. Lionesses from one family padded away from the lions and cubs. They dropped to their stomachs and crept toward the river.

"What are they doing, Gwamma Egyptus?" Rivka asked from her arms, pointing toward the lionesses.

"They are going to —" Ami said.

Egyptus touched the older girl's arm. "Watch, dear. This is the reason we are careful when the big cats are near."

Crouching low behind some rushes, the lionesses eyed a small herd of gazelles drinking from the edge of the river. One gazelle always stood with its head up, ears twitching, and eyes flicking from bush to bush. On some unknown signal, another gazelle would lift its head and the first would drop its head to drink.

Even with the careful protectiveness of the adult gazelles, the lionesses inched closer until they were less than the length of the shortest lioness from the gazelles.

"Gwamma!" Rivka gasped. "They are too close to those gazelles."

"Watch," Egyptus said, meeting Ami's eyes to remind her to stay quiet.

As one gazelle dropped his head and another lifted hers, the lionesses sprang forward toward one of the bigger gazelles.

Rivka sucked in her breath. "Will they catch it?" she whispered.

"The lions need to eat as much as we and the gazelles do. Observe what they do." Egyptus's stomach tightened, knowing what would happen.

The lionesses spread out, chasing the gazelle from different directions. The claws of a lioness grazed his rump. He jumped and raced away. The lionesses converged on the gazelle.

All the other gazelles raced up the river, but the one targeted by the lionesses ran down river.

Before the gazelle could run far, the lionesses caught him, leaping at him from all directions.

"Gwamma! He is bleeding!" Rivka cried. She buried her face in Egyptus's neck.

One lioness gripped the gazelle's throat. Another landed on its hindquarters, running along behind the gazelle with her claws and teeth clinging to it.

Lionesses raced on either side, leaping on to take the place of the one that fell away. Soon the gazelle slowed, dripping blood from its neck, back, and hind legs.

"Can we help it?" Rivka asked, tears flowing from her eyes.

"No, dear. The lions and their cubs need food too. They are here to protect us. We cannot keep them from eating when their food is near." Egyptus patted the girl's shoulder.

Rivka's eyes riveted on the attacking lionesses.

"It is not a pretty sight, but it is something you should see. Each animal must find food for themselves and their babies. Your papa hunts for animals when we need more than the Black River brings. Jehovah provides us with animals to eat. He gave the lionesses the knowledge to hunt for their food as well."

"It is sad," Ami said, touching her sister's leg. "But they need to eat. Watch."

The lioness that had clung to the gazelle's neck dragged it toward the place where her lion family lay. The gazelle was big enough she had to straddle the animal to drag it.

"The lioness must be tired," Ami said. "She is not moving fast."

"It takes a long time and a lot of effort to catch your food," Egyptus said. "We may have missed another attempt to bring down food for their family. Those lionesses are tired and still have much to do."

A second lioness took the gazelle from the first and dragged it toward their family. Others ran beside it, taking a turn when necessary to drag the gazelle through the bush to their family.

As they neared the lion family, the cubs jumped from beside the big lions and ran toward their mamas. One lioness swatted the cubs away. The lions stood and lazily moved toward the lionesses and the gazelle. The lioness dropped the gazelle and stepped back. The largest lion straddled the gazelle and tore into its bloody throat. Other lions joined him, tearing into the carcass. The lionesses waited before joining the lions. Cubs stood mewling from the edge of the circle of lions and lionesses ripping meat away from the bones of the gazelle.

Little Rivka watched, tears flowing down her face. "When will the cubs get to eat?"

"Observe," Ami said. "They will get their turn."

The big lions moved away from the half-eaten gazelle and lay on the grass, licking their paws. The cubs rushed in to rip away the last of the muscle attached to the bones. The lionesses pulled the bones apart and chewed on them.

"One gazelle did not give the lion family much to eat," Ami said.

"No. But it was enough for now. The lionesses will hunt again tomorrow," Egyptus said.

"Why do those lazy lions not help?" Rivka asked. "Papa and our brothers help mama with the hard work."

Egyptus patted her back. "They do. But your papa and brothers are people, made in the image of Jehovah. They know to help your mama. Lions are different. Lions protect the cubs and lionesses from other lions. The lionesses show their gratitude by feeding the lion."

"Do the tiger and leopard mamas feed the papa cats?" Ami asked.

"We will have to watch them to see," Egyptus answered, pointing toward tigers slinking toward the gazelle herd who had returned to drink from the river.

"I thought tigers hunt alone?" Ami asked.

"Usually they do. But sometimes they come together for the hunt. Being here around our village is different for them." Egyptus set Rivka on the walkway. "The big cats rarely gather as they have done since Ludim and his friends attacked us. I suspect the tigers and leopards changed their normal hunting patterns while they gathered to protect us."

"How long will the cats stay here to keep our enemies away?" Ami asked.

"I do not know," Egyptus said, staring out at the tigers who continued to creep toward the gazelles. "They will stay here as long as Jehovah keeps them here."

"It is good we do not have to worry about being attacked by wandering men while the cats are here," Esrom said, approaching his sisters and grandmama from the other end of the walkway. "I do not mind watching for men who do not come. But I do not like fighting against them, especially those who were once family."

A gazelle leapt high as the herd raced away, struggling to escape the tigers. A tiger snatched it from the air, clamping its jaws around the gazelle's neck. Rivka squealed from beside Egyptus and gripped her hand.

Other tigers aimed for smaller gazelles, chasing and dragging them to the earth, while some focused on others when the original gazelle escaped. Each tiger in the group dragged its prey back to the section of land where their cubs lay waiting.

The tiger families tore into the gazelles. They would eat well that night.

With a sigh, Egyptus took Ami's hand. "Time to return to our home. We still have chores to do."

Ami groaned but walked with her grandmama and sister down the stairs and toward their home.

Ami and Rivka squeaked as rain fell on them and their grandmama before reaching their front door. Ami pulled her hand from Egyptus's grip and raced down the path toward her home.

"Do not forget to clean the mud from your shoes," Egyptus called after her.

"Why must we clean our shoes?" Rivka asked.

"Because your mama spends much time on her knees washing her floors. You would not want her to be sad," Egyptus said.

"Or angry. She shouts when we make a mess of her clean floors! I will clean my shoes and take them off."

"Smart girl, Rivka."

They scurried through the rain, stopping only to rub the mud from their shoes on the low-growing greenery that grew in front of Xenia's and Pharoah's home. Stopping at the step, they scraped the last of the mud on a rock that stood beside the door for that purpose. Both Rivka and Egyptus removed their shoes and left them on the porch beside the door.

"Mama, we are home!" Rivka called as she bounced through the door.

The fragrance of a stew cooking over the fire filled the house. Xenia looked up from her comfortable seat in the sitting room and set her mending in her lap. "Did you enjoy your outing with your grandmama?"

"You will never believe it, Mama. We watched lionesses kill a gazelle!" the little girl cried.

"Then we saw tigers kill several more. Why did the gazelles not find another place to drink or move up the river? They stayed near the river where the tigers could take them. I would have crossed the river or moved further up the river if I were being attacked by tigers and lions," Ami said as she bounced onto a seat with her mending basket in her hands.

"Did you not see what waited for them in the river?" Egyptus asked.

Rivka stared up at her grandmama, who sat in a chair and helped herself to mending. "Why could they not cross the river? What kept them on this side?"

"Crocodiles. If you had looked closer, you would have seen their brown and green bodies floating in the river." Egyptus chose a tunic with a split seam and found a needle and thread in the basket.

"Mama Egyptus, you do not need to do my mending," Xenia said, winking at Ami.

Egyptus grinned. "No. I do not need to help, but I prefer to help while I sit here with you and your girls. I do not have mending waiting for me at my house." She threaded her needle and tied a knot.

"I thought those were logs!" Ami said, pulling a dress from her mending basket and stitching the hem.

"They lay in the water pretending to be logs, so unsuspecting animals will run across the river into their wide jaws," Xenia said. She examined the tunic she mended, searching for more loose seams.

"The gazelles must have seen them there," Ami said. "I saw a mama gazelle turn her little one away from the river. I wondered why they did not escape across it. But why not race downriver?"

"Leopards waited there for them," Egyptus said, stabbing her sharp needle into the seam. "They had cats on land wanting to take them for food and crocodiles waiting for them to blunder into the water. They had the poor gazelles trapped. I am surprised so many of them escaped."

"Why does Jehovah allow the wild cats to eat gazelles?" Ami asked, her needle suspended in the air as she stared at her grandmama.

"He knows the wild cats need to feed their young and themselves, as we must. He allows them to use their cunning and hunting skills to chase down and kill animals for food. None of the cats took more than they could eat. They will eat what is left tomorrow, or share them with the hyenas and birds. Those big cats do not waste food."

"Not like some children I know," Xenia said, grinning at Egyptus.

"Yes. Some children need to learn to eat what they take," Egyptus agreed with a nod.

"Mama gives me too much food," Rivka whined.

"You need to learn to eat and stop playing," Xenia said.

Egyptus laughed. "I remember saying the same things to my children. Do you think the mama tigers, lions, and leopards ever growl at their cubs?"

"Stop playing with your food and eat!" Ami said with a giggle.

"If you do not stop playing, you will be hungry later," Rivka chortled.

"I can hear the mama cats now," Egyptus said, laughing with the girls.

"Eat your food or I will not feed you tomorrow," Xenia said, joining the gaiety.

The four of them giggled as all but Rivka stabbed needles into the clothing they mended.

"When is Rivka going to learn to mend?" Ami asked.

"Her hands are still small ..." Egyptus said.

"I can mend my baby clothing," Rivka said.

"I will give you some fabric to sew together. You can practice sewing pieces together and make your baby a blanket," Xenia said. "Would you like that?"

The little girl brightened. Xenia set her mending aside and took Rivka into her workroom to search for fabric. They returned with several squares of bright linen. Xenia threaded a needle and showed her small daughter how to stab the needle in and pull the thread through tight enough to hold without puckering the fabric.

"I remember teaching my girls to sew," Egyptus said. "It is one thing we pass on to our children."

"Who taught you, Grandmama?" Ami asked.

"My mama, Basya. Her mama taught her, and each mama taught the next to sew all the way back to Eve."

"Eve?" Ami asked. "Was Eve a real person? Some girls say she is a story, someone our mamas made up."

Egyptus exchanged a look with Xenia. "That has been the story the Destroyer has tried to teach since families first moved away from Home Village," Egyptus said. "He wants us to forget about our first parents, Eve and Adam. He wants us to forget Grandpapa Noah and Grandmama Imma. If we forget them, the Destroyer believes we will forget about Jehovah. If we forget Jehovah, the Destroyer can teach his lies."

"Do you know anyone who knew Eve?" Ami persisted.

"She died many years before Grandmama Imma was born. Not even Grandpapa Noah knew our first parents, but his grandpapa knew them. My mama has a book Grandmama Eve wrote to tell her story. Of all the things Mama Basya could have taken on the ark, she insisted on bringing the books written by our first matriarchs."

"Did you read them?" Ami asked. "Where are they?"

"I read them often while I still lived in my mama's home. I do not know where they are now. I did not ask Mama for permission to bring them with me. They are too special to her. I suspect she carried them with her when she and Papa left Shinar."

"Would she carry heavy books with her?" Xenia asked.

"She would. She insisted they go with her on the ark. She would take them in her belongings when she left Shinar."

Floods

Three days later, Egyptus sat at her table writing the first words of a new copy of the Book of Commandments she planned to give to Levi and Lexa though their marriage rite would occur before she completed their copy. She would let them know she had started it for them on their marriage day.

She had given Animim his copy the day before. He had wept when he opened the scroll and read from it.

"I did not expect this," he had said through his tears.

"You earned it," Egyptus said, rubbing the back of her neck, embarrassed her gift brought him to tears. "You brought me many more papyrus reeds than any of the others who received books. Will Gilit allow you to keep it?"

"I am the patriarch of our family. I can read, so I will keep it and read it often. She does not need to know that I have a copy. She should have learned."

Egyptus shook her head, remembering his reaction to it. She hoped Gilit left it alone. It would not be beyond her to burn the scroll because she could not read it.

As she set her pen into the ink to write more words, twelve-year-old Iram bounced into her small home. "Papa sent me to get you. There is something you need to see."

She set her pen in the cup and pushed her chair back. "Where is he?"

"On the walkway. He said you should hurry." Iram tugged at her arm.

"Is it that important?"

"Papa thought it was."

Egyptus grabbed her cloak from the peg behind her door to wear in case of rain, then followed her grandson toward the wall. She marveled at how tall he had grown in the past weeks. He would be a man before she was ready. When would she ever be ready for her grandchildren to become adults?

"Not so fast, Iram," she called. "I am an old woman."

He stopped and turned, setting his fists on his hips. "Not so old, Grandmama. You are still young."

"Do you think so? You can run faster than me." She caught his arm and tucked her hand into the crook of his elbow.

Iram hurried away with her in tow, only a little slower than before. "You fought the last attackers and captured some of them. You must still be young."

"Because I practice with my staff every morning. Do you practice with your sword?"

Red crept up Iram's neck. "No, Grandmama. Papa keeps me busy. Besides, it rains in the morning."

"If you want to join the warriors on the wall, you need to practice with your weapons, even in the rain. Do you expect the enemy to attack only on sunny days?"

They reached the stairs to the walkway. Iram stepped back so Egyptus could climb them first. "That is what Papa tells me. I will join the men in the morning."

"You will be happy you did," Egyptus said before she hurried up the stairs to meet her son.

Pharoah leaned against the wall above the gate and stared out into the mists. "You came fast. Iram must have forced you to run."

"No, but he tried," Egyptus said with a laugh. "What is it you want me to see? The cats are still prowling out there."

"Good thing." Pharoah pointed out past the big cats. "There. Do you see them?"

Egyptus stared in the direction he pointed. "What am I seeing?"

"Movement."

She squinted her eyes to see better. Dark shadows ducked from one tree to the next. "Those moving shadows?"

She saw Pharoah nod out the corner of her eye. "What is it?"

"Men."

"Men?" her voice rose on the word. She swallowed. "Who?"

It could not be Ludim with all these cats. Could it? No.

Pharoah's shrug was small enough Egyptus nearly missed it. "The distance and the mists shroud them. I can only tell it is people, not animals. I suspect it is your friend."

Egyptus jerked her head toward Pharoah. "My friend? Who would that be? I have few friends who do not live inside these protective walls."

Her son put an arm around her and pulled her close. "That was mean. I apologize. I suspect it is Ludim and his friends ... no, companions. I do not believe he has any friends."

"Not if he treats everyone like he treated us," Egyptus said with a little shake of her head. "Who can befriend someone who constantly screams and complains?"

"Some must have, for there is more than one man out there." Pharoah pointed with his chin and released her from his embrace.

Three shadows ran from the cover of bushes, disappearing behind a stand of trees.

"It could be others who are trying to find a way around the wild cats that have made their home here," Egyptus said. She did not know whether to hope the men were new to Egypt or that they were those she and the women in her squad had defeated earlier.

"It could be, but —" Disbelief colored Pharoah's voice. "I do not believe even our worst enemies would try to attack us in this rain. It is too muddy and slippery to attack an unknown enemy."

"It does not matter who it is. All were once part of our family. Sadly, we must now consider all strangers as enemies until they prove they are not. Sad. I prefer to think about it the other way."

"We tried to consider them as friends in need," Pharoah reminded her. "They preferred to attack us when they could not comprehend our words."

"Those people did not understand everything that can happen when Jehovah finally curses a people. Not being able to perceive the words others say causes great fear and distrust." Egyptus sighed at her remembered dream. "Even if those people were once neighbors, friends, and family, we cannot immediately trust them until they prove themselves to be friendly."

"Not anymore. Each time we encounter another group of wanderers, they prove their troublesome natures," Pharoah added.

They watched the men dodging between trees and bushes in the distance for several breaths.

"What do you plan to do about those men?" Egyptus asked.

"That is why I sent Iram to get you, Mama," Pharoah said, turning toward her. "What do you think we should do about them?"

"Do you think they can get past the cats?"

Pharoah gazed at the big cats lolling in their family groups near the walls. The lions, tigers, cheetahs, and jaguars, along with other wild cats, kept their distance from other family groups.

"Probably not today. But the cats will not stay here forever, and we do not want them to stay here. We will need to plant our fields outside the walls. What do we do then?"

Egyptus allowed her gaze to flow from the wild cats to the fields, now covered with flood waters. Some green poked above the water. The floods had not covered the fields with their fertile black mud and the harvest was smaller than it had been in the years before. She hoped the black mud now settled over the grains.

"We will need to get past the cats to plant and harvest. And we will need to fish and gather papyrus," she said.

Pharoah nodded. "Yes. I wonder if Jehovah will send the cats away then. I am certain he brought them here to protect us."

"I am grateful He did. How many enemy groups have passed by Egypt since the cats came?"

"We cannot tell how many passed during the night or who saw our walls and skirted around us. We have counted fifteen groups who marched close to our walls until they saw the wild cats."

"Fifteen? I did not know there were that many."

Pharoah nodded. "We are blessed to have the cats lying about near our walls. But what do we do if it floods up the hill to our walls? The cats will leave us then. They dislike water."

Egyptus could not hide the shudder that shook her. "Flood water will keep our enemies away. Then what? The cats will be gone when the floods recede."

"We will need men to watch for enemies night and day, but not our children. Ami and Iram can warn us of their nearness, but they are too young and untrained to fight."

Egyptus turned her stare on her son. "You think they would take our children?"

"For slaves? Yes. Our daughters taken as their wives? Absolutely. Those men act like they have not had the softening touch of a woman for a long time. They must have lost their wives and families. Even if they did not, they will want our girls for wives and slaves."

Egyptus did not bother to hide the shiver that shook her body.

She nodded at the men skirting the wild cats in the distance. "There is little we can do about those men today. We are no more able to go out to them than they can come to us. The cats are doing their job."

"We will continue to keep a guard watching," Pharoah said. His gaze turned south beyond the ridge of hills. "Clouds are gathering. It may flood again soon."

"Water will keep strangers away."

"For a few days. But once the cats are gone, we will be forced to guard our walls, our village, and our families once more on our own."

Flood waters from the river gradually rose toward the walls of Egypt the next day. By midday, some of the wild cats had deserted the hill surrounding the walls, escaping the rising waters.

Egyptus joined the others in a special meeting Pharoah had called. When everyone had settled in front of him, he stood.

"The cats have blessed us while they stayed close. They have protected us from outside invaders."

Egyptus allowed a soft sigh to escape as Pharoah gazed around the room.

"That is ending. The rains in the south are bringing more floods. The waters rise. Already, many of the wild cats have left to avoid being drowned. I left some young people on the wall today to watch for any enemies while we discuss our current problem."

Murmurs rose from the crowd. Pharoah allowed them to settle into their seats and quiet before he continued.

"We will need men on the walkways to guard our village day and night."

"Enemies cannot pass the flood waters," Levi said. "Why would we need a guard?"

Pharoah ran a hand through his hair. "Because the flood has not yet reached our walls. Until they do, we cannot depend on the water keeping enemies away. Even then, they may reach our walls and attack us, especially if we are not watchful."

"Are there men out there? It has rained recently. Why would men want to attack us now?" Gilit called.

It would be Gilit who asked that.

"We saw men running between the bushes and trees in the distance yesterday," Egyptus said. "Even with the wild cats surrounding our walls, there were at least three men seeking to find a way around them."

"Why would you have seen the men, Egyptus?" Gilit said, a sneer filling her voice. "Women do not guard our walls."

Before Egyptus could respond, Pharoah answered. "I asked my mama to join me on the wall yesterday. I wanted her opinion."

"What could *that* woman —" Gilit demanded.

But Pharoah interrupted her. "It is not your problem. It is my choice to counsel with whomever I choose. If I choose to ask you, no one will question me."

A low rumble filled the room.

"As I said before, we will need men to guard the walls. Which team is willing to be first? We will take watches of four spans for now. No one will be there too long, and every team will have a turn before the water reaches our walls and closes us in. It is the back that will need guarding the most. Discuss this in your group. We will reconvene after you decide."

The men discussed the problem while the women sat quietly listening. They had not requested the women to stand guard on the wall since they had responsibility for children and homes.

I could stand on the wall as easily as the men, but I will not volunteer. That would give Gilit more of a reason to complain.

After a time, the men returned a few at a time to sit with their wives. When all had returned, Jakob stood. "My team will take the first watch."

Others claimed the next watch until all the men had assignments.

"Thank you," Pharoah said. "We need to be vigilant even in the rain. We do not know if it will flood enough to cover the land surrounding our village walls. We still have a few cats out there, but as the water reaches the land they have claimed, they are leaving."

"Then why —?" Gilit interrupted.

"We cannot depend on them to stay out there with the floods rising. Those big cats will protect their young as we do."

Pharoah stared harshly at Gilit, then gazed around the room. "Any more questions?"

No one raised a question.

"Let us pray. Then you are excused. Do not forget your assignment to guard against the enemy."

Problems

A large yellow cat ran from the trees as Egyptus walked home. It bumped its head up against her leg, searching for attention. She bent down to stroke it.

"Hello Buttercup. Where have you been? I have not seen you in several days." She lifted the cat into her arms and stood.

Buttercup purred beneath her hand, then meowed.

"Did you slip out to visit your cousins, the big cats? They are big enough to think of you as food."

The cat continued to purr in her arms.

"Have you been out looking for food? I hope you plan to stay inside the wall now. The flood waters will reach us soon."

Buttercup purred again, then jumped from her arms. The cat ran a few steps ahead, then stopped, meowing at Egyptus.

Egyptus stopped walking toward her door. "Did you need something, Buttercup?"

The yellow cat ran to her, rubbed her body along Egyptus's legs, then moved purposely a few steps away. She stopped and stared back.

"Do you want me to follow you?" Egyptus took a hesitant step toward her cat. Buttercup ran a few more steps, then stopped and stared at Egyptus.

"I am coming. Remember, I cannot crawl beneath the brush."

Buttercup turned and hurried away, slowing occasionally to glance back, confirming that Egyptus still followed. The cat led the way with her tail standing up tall, bent only at the end. They passed behind Pharoah's home and three others before the cat turned toward the barn where they kept the cows. Buttercup jumped onto the gate, then down into the barn.

Egyptus unlatched the gate and stepped in, closing the gate behind her. No need to let the cows get out. Buttercup's tail twitched as she led Egyptus to a space behind a large basket of grain.

Egyptus squinted in the low light, trying to see why her cat had led her here. She stooped down as close as she could get to the back of the basket. "What do you have here, Buttercup?"

The cat lay down, curling around something. Tiny mewling sounded, then suddenly ended.

"Kittens? I should have known you would have kittens."

Buttercup stared up at her. Six tiny kittens lay at her side, nursing.

"You do have kittens! Good for you. We must increase our posterity. Who is the papa?"

Several families had brought cats with them on the journey to Egypt and most of the females had given birth in the three years. This was not her first litter, so any of them could have sired these kittens.

"Do you want me to bring the kittens home?"

Buttercup stood and the kittens dropped from her teats, mewling piteously.

"You are not that hungry," Egyptus cooed, lifting the kittens into her lap. Four were yellow like their mama. The other two had black stripes mixed in with the yellow. "So your papa had black in him?" she said, using a quiet voice.

She cradled the kittens in her skirt and carefully stood. Buttercup wound her body between Egyptus's legs, then headed toward the gate.

Buttercup walked beside Egyptus to her home, careful not to trip her. The cat ran through the door ahead of Egyptus and leapt onto a chair. Egyptus set the kittens in the chair with their mama.

"There you go, little ones. Your mama can feed you now. I will go find a basket for your little family, Buttercup."

The cat stared up and mewed softly. The kittens had already found her teats and were kneading her to increase the milk flow.

Egyptus grinned, then walked into her sleeping space, looking for a low basket to use for a bed. A basket made of papyrus sat empty in a corner. She lined the papyrus basket with two towels she found in a trunk, then carried it into the sitting room where the kittens still nursed.

When the kittens let go and lay next to their mama, Egyptus lifted them into the basket. Buttercup jumped into the basket, turned around three times, and curled around her kittens.

"This must work for you. I'll set it near the fire so your little ones do not get cold when you are gone." Egyptus slowly lifted the basket to the floor.

Buttercup meowed softly, then lay her head on her paws and closed her eyes.

"I know. It is hard to be a mama," Egyptus whispered before standing and moving to her table. She still had many chapters to copy for Levi and Lexa.

She found her place in the Book of Commandments, dipped her pen into the ink, sighed deeply, and wrote on the scroll once more.

When Buttercup cried softly at her kitchen door, Egyptus stood and stretched. She opened the door for the cat and looked out. The sun had almost set. She had lost herself in copying the text.

Men tromped through the village and along the lengths of the walkways, some stood gazing outward.

Questions filled her mind. Why were so many men on the walls when the flood waters would soon reach them? What did they see? Had the floods driven away all the big cats? Who were the men out there? She hoped Ludim had not tried to return.

Leaving her door slightly ajar to let Buttercup return and settle in with her kittens, Egyptus grabbed her cloak. If it rained again, she did not want to be caught without it. She hurried out the door toward the wall and the men.

Shiblom met her as she reached the steps to the walkway. "What brought you out?"

"I saw men on the walls. What is happening? Did Ludim return?"

Shiblom shook his head. "No. He could not get through all the water out there if he wanted."

"Why is everyone alert?" Egyptus asked. She climbed the stairs to see what was happening for herself. As she reached the top, men moved aside.

"I have never seen the water rise this high," Emer said, stepping aside so she could stand next to him.

She leaned on the wall and stared out at the rising water. It already reached the edge and crept higher.

"Did all the big cats escape before the water surrounded us?" she asked.

"As far as I know," Arvad said from her other side.

"I saw the last big cat leave as the waters closed around us," Pharoah said.

"I suspect the cat listened to Jehovah as it waited until it was almost too late," Egyptus said. She leaned over the wall to see how close the water came.

"Be careful, Mama!" Pharoah said. "You do not want to fall into the water."

"No, but I want to see how close the water has come to the wall," Egyptus said, standing back from the edge of the wall.

"It laps against all our walls," Shiblom said, "and it does not look like it will stop rising soon."

"That could be a problem," Egyptus murmured.

"A big problem," Pharoah agreed. "The wall will not be safe if the water continues to rise."

"We cannot stop the water, but Jehovah can. We must ask Him for help." Egyptus turned from the wall and headed for the stairs.

Men followed her down the stairs, then strode purposefully toward their homes to gather their wives and children. Egyptus crossed the gathering place to the sanctuary with Iram and Adok, who had stood on the walkway with the men. The boys moved the seats into place so the others would have seats when they arrived.

Soon the others trickled into the sanctuary, speaking in low voices. Their fear spread through the room. Egyptus took several deep breaths before she moved through the room to speak to the families.

"Do not fear," she said to each family. "Jehovah brought us here. He will not allow the flooding river to destroy us. We must pray for His help and trust Him to protect us."

Mamas soothed their children. Papas hugged their wives and murmured in gentle voices to their family as they moved into the room and took seats. Fear crept out the door, replaced by hope and trust.

When Pharoah and Xenia arrived with their younger children, Pharoah helped them find a place among the others. Then he stepped to the front of the room, looking around to ensure everyone had arrived. Before he spoke, Animim and Gilit slipped through the back door and sat at the back. Egyptus took her seat near the front on the end and waited to hear what Pharoah had to say.

"As you may have heard, we have a problem," Pharoah said. He waved an arm toward the wall. "The river has flooded. Our walls are at risk."

"The river rises to the wall every year. How is this different?" Animim asked.

"It has, and the wall has kept the water out each year since we put stones around the base of the wall," Pharoah said.

"So what is the problem?" Gilit asked. Her snarl echoed through the room.

Could the woman ever support Pharoah?

"The water rose faster than it ever has, and it does not look like it will stop. If you look at the sky to the south, you will see thick black clouds dropping rain on that land." Pharoah's patience with the woman continued to surprise Egyptus.

"What do you expect for us to do? We can do nothing here in the sanctuary," Gilit grumbled.

"We can pray. Only Jehovah can protect our walls and our homes. We need to pray and ask for His help," Pharoah replied.

"In earlier times," Egyptus said, waving her hand back, "people fasted when they were in great need."

"What is fasting?" Bilhah asked.

"But what is fasting?" Ami asked, almost echoing her older sister.

Egyptus glanced at her granddaughters, then around the room. Many of the faces of her loved ones showed confusion. She patted Ami's arm. "Fasting means you go without food while you pray for help from Jehovah."

Ganet gasped. "Until the waters disperse? That could be days or weeks!"

"Only for a few days. You fast from sunup to sundown." Egyptus stared around the room. "However, Jehovah does not expect those of you carrying unborn babes or nursing mamas to fast like that. That would be dangerous for your little ones. We cannot expect little children to not eat or drink either."

"I can fast," Rivka said, poking out her lower lip.

Egyptus hugged the little girl. "You can miss one meal, or eat less than you usually eat. You need food to grow."

"We will see," the little girl said.

"I have read about fasting," Pharoah said. "Jehovah has commanded us to fast when in great need. Mama is correct. We should fast. However, little children, nursing mamas, and women carrying unborn children should not fast as fully as the rest of us."

"But I have our evening meal nearly prepared," Angetta said. "When do you want us to begin this fast?"

"Is this the only solution? Is there something else we can do to stop the rain?" Shim asked.

"Do you have a suggestion?" Pharoah asked. "Does anyone have another suggestion?"

He stood gazing around the room, waiting.

With no other suggestions offered, he continued, "We must first decide if all members of our community will participate. It will do no good if some are not willing." Pharoah gazed around the room. "Are you all willing to fast?"

"For how long?" Rebecca asked.

"We will fast for three days, from sunrise until sunset," Pharoah answered. "Each day we will pray with our families, then come together morning and night to pray for the rains and flooding to dissipate, and for our walls to withstand the water. Are there any comments or other opinions?"

"We can eat after the sun sets?" Xenia asked.

"One small meal. That is the way I understand the things I read in the Book of Commandments. Is that what you remember, Mama?"

"Why do you always turn to your mama?" Gilit's strident tones filled the room. "She is not the only one who has lived with leaders of the family. Animim and Jakob could give you advice."

Egyptus waved her hand toward the men.

Pharoah turned to them. "Animim? Jakob? Moren? Do you remember fasting in the days before we left Shinar?"

Good. He should ask those men for their opinions.

Animim patted Gilit's arm and stood. "We did not have long fasts in the days we lived in Shinar that I remember. But I remember having fasts for a day to honor and worship Jehovah. Egyptus is correct about women with child and those others. They could modify their fast, but not go entirely without food and water for as long as the rest of us."

"Jakob, do you remember?" Pharoah asked.

Jakob stood. He glanced at Animim and Gilit. "Like Animim, I only remember one day fasts. However, we may need to fast longer than three days. I agree we should fast the three days, then determine if we need to continue." Jacob sat next to Chana, who took his hand in hers.

"Thank you," Pharoah said. "Moren, do you have anything to add?"

Isa and Moren spoke in soft tones to each other before Moren spoke. "I agree. We must fast now if we are to have protection from the flood. Those women who are with child can join us, but should only fast one meal each day and not go without water. Isa reminds me that mamas who carry unborn children and those who are nursing need water and other drinks to support their children. It may be best for them to eat smaller meals rather than not eating at all."

Moren sat. Isa set her hand on his knee. People in the room murmured their agreement to the things the three men had said.

Pharoah allowed them to discuss among themselves before calling them to order again.

"We need to take a vote. Do you agree to fast during the day for the next three days? If you do, please stand."

Egyptus waited a breath to see who would support this suggestion.

Xenia and her younger children rose. Egyptus joined them and glanced around the room. Slowly at first, the congregation rose. A few stubbornly sat. Even they stood as Pharoah waited, allowing them to decide, until only Gilit sat. She tugged on Animim's hand, trying to get him to sit as well.

"No, Gilit," he whispered loud enough for all to hear. "I believe we should all fast. If you choose not to join us, that is your right. I choose to be a part of this community and do what is best for us."

Gilit frowned as she stood. "I guess I must, since you are."

Not the best way to agree. Will it be enough?

"Do not agree to fast if you do not intend to do so willingly," Pharoah said. "But if you choose to do so, we appreciate you joining us. We should now kneel to pray."

Fasting

The next morning, Egyptus stood on the wall staring toward the south. She had prayed at home alone before joining the others in the sanctuary to beg Jehovah to halt the rain.

Now she stared at the black clouds that continued to loom over the land to the south. Egyptus sighed.

"It continues to rain," Moren said, walking from the corner where he watched for problems.

"It does. I knew it would take a while for the rains to stop there, but I hoped Jehovah would honor our prayers and fasting. Perhaps He is testing us."

"Perhaps. I did not expect the floods to end yet, but I thought maybe the rains would slow."

Egyptus lifted a shoulder. "We cannot see the rain there, only the clouds. Perhaps it has slowed."

"I pray it is so." Moren leaned on the edge of the wall, staring down into the floodwaters.

"Is your land flooded? Will Isa lose her herbs and other plants?"

Moren sighed and set his head into his hand, elbow leaning on the wall. "She may. She brought many of her plants here before the first rains came weeks ago. She left some in the ground there, expecting lower flood waters this year. But the water looks higher than I have ever seen it before. She will not be happy."

Egyptus leaned on the wall next to Moren. "It will sadden many of us if she loses her herbs and other plants, especially if someone needs healing."

"Isa is concerned about that as well."

Egyptus gazed up at the sky above the river in the south. Black clouds hung low over the land. She sighed. "We need to find a way to protect your land and the land of others who need to live on their land. We cannot suffer the destruction these floods cause every year."

"But we need the life-giving mud they bring to our fields." Moren waved his hand toward the wheat fields. "They grow better when they receive mud from the south."

"There must be a way to have the flood waters cover the fields and still avoid having them cover the rest of the land." Egyptus ran her hand through her hair. "We need to think and pray about it."

"Until we discover the solution, we should continue to fast and pray for this flooding to end." Moren stood tall. "Isa will want to know about her gardens."

"Give her my love," Egyptus said as he started down the steps.

Egyptus settled her chin into her hand and stared out at the muddy water. It lapped against the wood of the wall in every direction. How did the wall fare?

She tromped down the steps to examine the wall. Trickles of water leaked through the seams in the wall above the rocks they had placed during that first year of flooding. As she walked along the wall, she noticed some trickles were becoming streams. Homes close to the wall would soon be in danger of flooding if the southern rains did not end soon.

How could they stop the water from climbing the hill to the settlement or onto the other parcels of land? Families needed to move out into their own land sometime. They could not with the threat of flooding and enemy attacks. Double problems.

I will have to think and pray about this. Perhaps if I share the problem, someone else will come up with a solution.

After walking along the base of the wall and returning to the stairs near the gate, Egyptus turned back toward her home. She had things to do.

First, she would need to warn Pharoah about the leaks in the wall. Then ... Then what? She considered starting bread and a soup, but she was fasting. It would not be good to smell soup cooking during the day. She would have time to spend with Jehovah as she copied His words onto a scroll for Levi and Lexa.

Egyptus stopped at Pharoah's home long enough to warn him of the sprouting leaks in the wall. He thanked her, and she left. He and the men could resolve this problem on their own.

She retrieved her copy of the Book of Commandments and the scroll she had been working on to give to Levi and Lexa. She had less than a month before their marriage rite. She hoped to complete the scroll before then. Levi had worked hard to complete their new home. It would not be long before it would be ready for them.

Egyptus grinned at the thought. Lexa would be a beautiful bride.

She lit a candle and picked up her pen and wrote the words she had spent so long trying to remember as they crossed the wilderness to their new home. The memory of Afra's visit still warmed her soul as she completed writing what she remembered from her mama's book.

"Are you still with me, Afra?" she whispered. "I need you. What can we do to stop the flood waters from destroying our land? Help me know what we can do."

A breath of a breeze rustled through her hair and across her cheek. She lifted her hand to her face.

"You are here. What can we do? The floods have never risen so high."

Her candle flickered as the breeze wove around it. Afra heard her. Would he help with a solution?

She sat still, waiting for the breeze to brush past her face once more, but it did not return. At last, she slumped in her chair. The problem was hers. She would have to solve it on her own.

"If I think of a way, will you let me know if it is good?"

The breeze returned, brushing her cheek before slipping out the window.

I can think of a solution. I am intelligent and able. Between me and Jehovah, with Afra's help, we can solve this. But how?

Buttercup brushed past her legs, her soft fur tickling. She bent to lift the cat into her lap. Petting Buttercup, she thought about the need to stop the water.

Each morning and evening for three days, the members of the community gathered in the sanctuary for prayers. After the prayers, Egyptus and others traveled to the wall, hoping to see the flood waters receding.

The water had risen to the top of the rocks they had piled along the bottom of the walls. The stones filling the smaller holes now moved with the streamlets flowing between the logs. Puddles settled in depressions left by footprints. Egypt was in trouble.

Egyptus gazed toward the south with the others, expecting the clouds to have dissipated. She trusted Jehovah to honor their faith.

Black clouds still hung over the south lands on the evening of the third day.

"What did we do wrong?" Lexa asked. "We have fasted and prayed. Why has Jehovah not honored our prayers and stopped the rains in the south?"

"We cannot force Jehovah to bless us," Levi said before Egyptus could respond. He stood with his arm wrapped around Lexa. "Jehovah will give us the blessing that is good for us when it is right."

"Are you saying all this water is a blessing?" Lexa asked, her voice bordering on a shriek.

"Do you have faith that Jehovah will bless us?" Egyptus asked. "You cannot have questions or doubts. None of us can if we expect Jehovah to stop the rain."

"None of us?" Lexa asked.

"Why do you ask?" Egyptus asked. "Do you trust Jehovah?"

"I do. I know he will bless us. But ..."

"But?" Levi asked. "But what?"

"I live next to Animim and Gilit," Lexa said, dragging out her words. "I hear her talking to her dog in the back of her house while I work in our garden." She chewed on her lip and glanced both directions.

"She is not here," Levi said.

"Are you certain?" Lexa asked. She turned and glanced at the men who stood on the wall gazing at the flood waters and clouds. "She does not expect the rains to end. She said something ..."

"Something?" Egyptus asked, hoping to encourage the young woman to share.

"She told her dog not to tell the others, but she would not fast, only feign her fast. She does not think Jehovah can stop the rain."

Egyptus's eyebrows leapt to her hairline. "She does not believe Jehovah can control the rain?"

"That is what she told her dog. I can smell the food she cooks during the day. She gives some to that dog but told him she eats some herself."

Egyptus sucked in a deep breath and slowly allowed it to escape. *That could be our problem.*

She stared out until Levi and Lexa moved down the wall. Then she hurried down the steps and rushed to Pharoah's home.

Ami met her at the door. "Grandmama! I thought you were on the wall."

"I was. Is your papa home?"

Ami pulled the door open wide. "He is. Come in."

Ami led her toward Pharoah's and Xenia's sleeping space. "Papa is in there with Mama."

"Thank you, Ami. I have missed you these past days."

"I have taken care of Rivka and Bilhah's little Jon while Mama and Bilhah dyed the fabric they wove."

"Is it a nice color?" Egyptus asked, stopping outside the door to Pharoah's sleeping room.

"It is a beautiful blue, like the sky after rain."

"That sounds beautiful. What do they plan to make of their blue fabric?"

Ami shrugged. "I do not know. Mama and Bilhah refuse to tell me."

Egyptus gave her a brief hug. "They will tell you when you are ready."

"I know. Papa and Mama are in there."

Egyptus knocked softly on their door.

"Yes?" Pharoah called.

"It is me, your mama," Egyptus said. "May I enter?"

After a few short breaths, Pharoah opened the door, smoothing his tunic.

"I am sorry to interrupt," Egyptus said. "I would not if this was not important."

Pharoah glanced at Xenia. "Should we walk?"

"No. Xenia may help with this problem."

Pharoah opened the door wider to wave Egyptus through. "Then come in and sit."

Egyptus sat on the stool and faced Pharoah and Xenia. Frustration and defeat filled her. "I just left the wall. Dark clouds continue to hang over the south."

"I had hoped they would lift by now," Xenia said.

"I did as well," Egyptus said. "As I stared at the flood and the clouds, I learned something that may be the problem."

"Oh?" Pharoah asked, lifting his eyebrows.

"It seems not everyone who covenanted to fast has been fasting. There is one who is eating and does not believe Jehovah can stop the rain."

"Who?" Pharoah asked.

"I suspect I know," Xenia said, gazing at Egyptus. "Is it our friend who often causes problems?"

"Yes. Lexa lives in the house beside hers and heard her bragging to her dog that she does not believe Jehovah can help us. Lexa has smelled food cooking each day as we have been fasting. The woman told the dog she eats while the others fast, only feigning to join."

"How could she?" Pharoah asked. "We told her not to agree if she did not plan to participate. She has lied to us all."

"And endangered Egypt," Xenia said.

"What can we do?" Egyptus asked. "You are our leader. What can we do?"

Pharoah stood from the bed where he had been sitting beside Xenia and paced to the window, staring out for many breaths before pacing back. He sat once more and took Xenia's hand.

"I will need to discuss this with the elders."

"Will you tell Animim who is causing the problem?" Egyptus asked.

"I do not know. I suspect he knows already. I will go to Jakob, Moren, Meyer, and Animim and seek their counsel. We may be out late." He kissed Xenia, then brushed his lips against Egyptus's cheek before marching out the door of the sleeping room.

"What will happen to Gilit?" Xenia asked.

"I do not know," Egyptus said, shaking her head. "All I know is something must happen for Jehovah to bless us. We require a blessing, or the flood waters will wash away our village."

The Egyptians met early the next morning in the sanctuary to offer another prayer to Jehovah. Before inviting the congregation to kneel to pray, Pharoah stood in front with Moren and Jakob. Meyer and Animim sat on either side of them, ready to offer support.

"We," Pharoah said, indicating the five men, 'have something to discuss with you before we join in prayer this morning." He chewed on his lower lip before speaking again.

"We have a problem."

"We do. Dark clouds continue to cling to the land to the south of us," Arvad said. "I expected they would have lifted by now."

"We did as well," Jakob said. "We hoped our honest fasting and prayers would convince Jehovah to stop the rain. We agreed earlier that all would fast and pray."

"We have fasted!" Tama said. "Even my little ones have eaten less food, trying to fast honestly."

"We know," Moren said. "I have seen hunger on the faces of many children not old enough to fast."

"They insisted on fasting with us, to do their part to protect our home," Ganet said. "I could not force them to eat."

"Nor could I force my little ones," Bilhah said, while other mamas of young children nodded.

"What is the problem, then?" Chayim asked.

"Has someone not fasted as they agreed?" Kib asked.

"That would not happen," Rebecca said. "Would it?"

Pharoah sucked in a deep breath. "That is the problem. Someone here agreed to fast with the rest of us. But this person felt forced. This person did not choose to participate."

The members of the congregation turned to their neighbor, questioning who would not take part in the effort to get help from Jehovah. The buzz in the room sounded like hornets buzzing in anger at a disturbance to their hive. Egyptus sat in silence, listening to the noise, waiting to see how Pharoah and the other men would deal with the one. *That one! Why is it always her?*

Pharoah allowed them to express their frustration and concern before he called the meeting back to order. "Jehovah gave us agency to decide for ourselves," he continued. "We cannot force anyone to participate. It will not honor Him to force another into doing something unwanted.

For this reason, I will not ask for you to covenant your willingness to continue with the fast publicly. Some of you have fasted all you are able. Others may not have the faith."

The members of the congregation buzzed softer this time, some sitting, like Egyptus, quietly saying nothing.

"I appreciate your quiet introspection. This is an individual commitment. I need you to silently and individually covenant with Jehovah that you will join us in the fast for another two days. Only two more days. More than that will not be healthy for any of us."

"But if we choose not to join in, others will see and have disdain for our inability to continue," Dora, Emer's wife, said. She placed her hands protectively over her swollen stomach.

"No one will know if you fast or not if you join us for morning and evening prayers." Pharoah paused, gazing around at the gathered crowd. "But rather than endanger any of you and your standing in the community, we will only gather in our homes, not here in the sanctuary. We will not embarrass you if you choose not to fast or pray. That will be your own choice." Pharoah waved his hand toward the men on either side of him, "We have taken the matter to Jehovah and this is his answer. No one will consider you better or worse because of your choices."

"But the person —" someone called from the congregation. Egyptus refused to turn to gaze in the speaker's direction. She would not be a part of the speculation.

"We will not discuss those who may or may not have participated in the last three days. I suggest we all return to our homes and pray with our families."

Pharoah walked to where Xenia and their younger children sat and walked quietly with them from the sanctuary. Jakob walked into the congregation and took Chana's hand and followed Pharoah's family.

Meyer and Ada, Moren and Isa, and Animim and Gilit followed behind, not looking to see if others would follow.

Egyptus stood and followed them out the door. Magda reached out to take her hand as she passed. "Mama? Will you come pray with our family?"

She nodded and kept walking. Magda, Arvad, and their young children followed her out the door, saying nothing more.

When they reached their home, Magda opened the door wide to welcome Egyptus.

Arvad invited his children to join them in a family circle. "Mama Egyptus, please join us in prayer."

Egyptus knelt between two little ones and lifted her arms and repeated the words Arvad spoke in a simple and sincere prayer, begging Jehovah to still the rain in the south and protect their homes.

Near the end of the prayer, Egyptus's chest burned with the warmth of an answer from Jehovah. As she dropped her arms after the final amen, she wiped away the tears that leaked from her eyes.

"You feel it too, Mama?" Arvad asked.

"Yes, Arvad. Your simple prayer filled my heart. I feel Jehovah's presence near. The rains will end and we will discover a way to stop the floods from destroying our land."

"How will that happen, Grandmama?" Ros asked.

"I do not know now," Egyptus answered, hugging the boy. "All I know is that Jehovah will help us resolve this problem."

Serpent

Egyptus climbed the stairs to the wall surrounding Egypt later that afternoon. Hope filled her. She knew when she stared to the south, black clouds would no longer settle on the horizon.

Although the stench of dead animals bouncing against the wall threatened to gag her, she still took a deep breath and let it out slowly before she stepped to stand beside Isa.

"I trust Jehovah and that the dark clouds will be gone. Yet I am fearful to look. Tell me, are they lifted?" Egyptus shut her eyes to the sight.

"You are fearful, Egyptus? You who reminded us to fast and pray? You who keep us remembering Jehovah?" Isa teased.

"I am not always strong. I know the clouds will lift. I do not know if they will be gone yet. But I trust Him."

Isa poked Egyptus in the side with her elbow. "Then open your eyes and see."

Egyptus bit down on her lips slightly, then allowed her eyelids to separate. She turned to face south and blew out the breath.

"The clouds are not just lifted and white, they are ... they are gone! Jehovah has answered our prayers."

"Pharoah and the other men did the right thing to ask us to commit silently. It gave each of us the opportunity to search our souls, to see if we had honestly fasted and prayed for the benefit of all Egypt. I found I could do better."

"I did as well."

"You?" Isa asked.

Egyptus turned in time to see Isa's eyebrows hike up her forehead. "I am not perfect. I question. I fear. I need support. I miss my Afra. He would laugh at my fears. But only my pillow hears my words of confusion and grief."

"I am here for you, Egyptus," Isa said, wrapping an arm around her waist. "I will listen to your sorrows."

"You are busy preparing healing tinctures and salves. You do not have time to listen to a lonely old woman whine."

"I have never heard you whine, my friend. And if you do, you have a right. I can complain to Moren in the dark of the night or even in the bright sunlight of day in the confines of our home. Who do you have to share with?"

"Jehovah. Afra." Egyptus bit the side of her cheek, forcing the tears to remain inside rather than drip down her face.

"Exactly. Who will hug you and tell you that you are doing well or that you have a reason for your fears? Does Afra come to comfort you?" Isa tightened her grip on Egyptus's waist.

"Sometimes Afra comes to comfort me." Egyptus reached up to wipe away a stray tear that had escaped despite her efforts. "I feel him like a soft breeze."

"But he cannot hug you. You miss the comfort and love of your man."

Egyptus inhaled a deep, shuddering breath. "Yes. I miss my Afra. I miss him holding me in the night when I am afraid. I miss his encouragement."

"Since Rebecca married, you spend too much time alone," Isa said.

Egyptus stepped out of her friend's embrace. "Not so much. I visit one of my children or grandchildren almost every day. The grandchildren give the best hugs."

Isa set her fists on her hips. "Better than mine? I am offended."

"You know the love and hugs from a child are different. It is pure and innocent. They have no other purpose than pure love."

"And I do not?" Isa feigned hurt, gripping a handful of her dress near her heart.

"You have your reasons."

Isa held her frown for a breath before allowing a smile to brighten her face. "I do. I do not like to see you sad. You know that everyone here in Egypt loves you."

"Everyone?" Egyptus asked. "Now I know you are wrong. I know of one person who does not love me."

"She would rather be with her papa in Shinar."

"And she could not be with him even now, for her language would have changed and separated them."

"She does not understand how blessed she is to be here in Egypt. I have heard her complaints. Her life here is better than it would be." Isa's frown darkened her face.

"She will learn sometime. Somehow. I do not want to be the one to force that learning on her." Egyptus shook her head and lifted the hair off her neck. "The breeze stopped. It is hot and sticky without it."

Isa glanced at the water below them. "Especially with all this water. It will drain away into the Siddim Sea now."

Egyptus followed her friend's glance. The water had not dropped yet, but since the rain had stopped upriver, the floodwaters would soon recede.

"Do you think those men are still out there? The ones hoping to sneak past the big cats?"

Egyptus jerked her head up and stared at Isa. "Those men? Do you think they would still be out there?"

"The cats left us," Isa said with a shrug of her shoulders. "Perhaps the flood washed those men away."

Egyptus shook her head. "I would not hope the flood waters washed them away. I would rather they saw the water coming and left the area. I do not like to even think of them out there, waiting to climb our walls again."

"The floods have been a blessing for that. We have little reason to send so many men to the wall to watch for danger from our enemies."

"Now they must walk along the inside on the ground to watch for leaks," Egyptus said with a sigh. "We have had a rough year with strangers attacking and the exceptionally high waters."

"Too many of our brothers and cousins have forgotten we are family and only see us as a place to steal food and women. It is sad."

"It is. Since the confounding of their languages, they have forgotten about the love families have for one another. How could they forget Jehovah the way they have?"

Isa pushed away from the wall and stretched. "They were not obeying his commandments before we left. They wanted to escape Jehovah's wrath as they built their tower. They forgot Him long ago. We look like an easy target to them."

"They are wrong. We are not an easy target for anyone."

"No, we are not targets. We always fight back and we have injured or killed many of those who attack us. It is a blessing that they have not killed or taken any of our people in their attacks."

She brushed her hair back from her face. "Jehovah has blessed us. But for how long? When will we lose a life? We are a small group and cannot afford to lose any of our people. I pray nightly for His protection."

Isa stepped toward the stairs leading from the walkway. "The time will come when our people forget to trust Jehovah. I pray it will be many years before we lose any of our men or women in the battles with strangers."

Isa's words rang in Egyptus's ears as she turned and walked down the stairs. What could she do to help her people remember to trust Jehovah? She did not want them to become like the men who attacked her village so often.

She sighed and turned to go home.

Water slowly drained from around the village walls. When it had receded away from the walls on the outside, the men examined them, planning to replace all they could while the water protected them. The men found many broken and rotted timbers needing to be replaced. They carefully pulled out one log at a time and replaced it, never leaving the open space without a guard to keep serpents and wild creatures from slipping through the gap.

Egyptus and most of the young women continued to practice using their staffs early in the morning. As the men worked on replacing the fifth log, Gilit screamed.

Egyptus and others joined the men who rushed to where Gilit stood screaming, bouncing on her toes, and pointing at the ground.

Not another walking fish. That is not charitable.

"A serpent! A serpent!" Gilit screamed.

"Where?" Animim asked, searching the ground for evidence.

"There!" she pointed at a hole in the ground. "It slithered down that hole."

Egyptus stretched her neck to see from the edge of the crowd where she stood, balancing her staff on her toes. She hoped Gilit was wrong and there was no serpent. She did not like them any more than Gilit did.

"We will find the serpent," Pharoah said, striding to the center of the circle next to the hole Gilit had pointed to. "You other men must return to the wall and replace that log before other serpents and wild creatures sneak into our village."

The men grumbled but hurried away to complete their work on the wall. Animim pulled his sword from his side and stabbed it into the hole. Pharoah did not have his sword with him, as he had been carrying the new log to the wall. Xenia handed him her staff, and he joined Animim stabbing at the hole where Gilit said the serpent had disappeared.

Egyptus and other women stood in a loose circle around the hole watching the men when Dora squealed. "Get away from me!" She stabbed at the wet ground with her staff.

A serpent slithered away, seeking to escape the end of her staff.

The dissonant smell of fear wrapped around the women. Egyptus struggled against its debilitating power to prevent action. She and others joined the battle, stabbing at the serpent. Although the serpent twisted away, it could not escape the stabbing staffs of the women. After many breaths and many stabs and bashes, the serpent lay dead on the earth.

Gilit threw herself into Animim's arms, quivering. "Is it ... Is it ... Is it ... dead?" she stammered.

Egyptus could almost taste the bitterness of Gilit's dread.

"It is, thanks to these women. They beat it to death with their staffs," Animim said, pulling Gilit close. "Where is your staff? Do you not join the women as they practice each morning?"

Gilit toed the earth with her shoe. "Not this morning. I did not feel well enough to stab and spin and work hard."

"Are you ill every morning?" Egyptus murmured under her breath. *You never join us to prepare to protect our lives or our home. You expect us to protect you when ... Do not pursue this thought.*

"I heard you, Egyptus. Yes. I have been ill for many mornings," Gilit growled.

"Have you been to visit with Isa? She may have a tincture or other cure that would help you," Dara asked.

"I have not. I do not feel bad enough to go to the healer," Gilit said with a sniff.

"If you continue to feel unwell, you may want to visit with her," Egyptus said. "Shall I suggest you have a need?"

"No." Gilit stomped a foot. "I will go to her if I need."

"It is your choice," Egyptus said, lifting a shoulder, then walked toward her home.

Dara and Elsa hurried after her. "She could have thanked us," Dara said when they had turned a corner and Gilit could no longer hear her.

"She never offers gratitude, only complaints," Elsa said. "It is hard to be around her."

"Do not allow her actions and attitudes to affect you," Egyptus said. "I remember reading in Eve's book about how hard it is to avoid the

Destroyer. When we do or say bad things about others, we become like him. Do not be like the Destroyer."

"I will not be like him," Dara and Elsa said together.

"It is hard to avoid the hatred of the Destroyer in this world. We must fight against it. We cannot allow Gilit to pull us into her sad and lonely world."

Egyptus gave each of her granddaughters a hug, enjoying the sweet fragrance of the babies they carried with them before leaving them to return to her own home. She still had pages to copy in the scroll for Levi and Lexa.

She sat at the table and lit the candle to brighten her work. The pungent tang of the papyrus mixed with the sweetness of the berries in her ink and the earthy fragrance of the candle. She unrolled her copy of the scroll, found her place, dipped her pen into the ink, and began to write.

The words Adam wrote in the Book of Commandments soothed her frustrated heart, even as she struggled with frustration and anger. If she was honest with herself the frustration and anger were with Gilit. Her anger and bad temper, combined with her unwillingness to be part of the community, made it difficult for Egyptus to forgive the woman. But she refused to give in to the hatred that the Destroyer encouraged.

Jehovah's words warmed her heart as she copied them. Gilit would be responsible for her actions and beliefs. Egyptus would not.

Buttercup walked past her legs, rubbing her soft body against Egyptus's legs. She bent to brush her hand across the cat's back and lifted it to her lap. Stroking Buttercup's fur, her thoughts turned to the serpent slithering at her feet, seeking to avoid the threat of their beating staffs. It only sought to escape the waters that threatened to drown it. How could it know of the fear of the women within the walls of Egypt?

She closed her eyes and offered a prayer to Jehovah, asking him to forgive her hatred of the serpent. She felt the peace of forgiveness before she set Buttercup on the floor and returned to her writing.

Testing Boats

A lma stopped by to visit with Egyptus two days later as she finished writing the last words on the scroll for Lexa and Levi. Egyptus had spent many hours bent over the scroll, lovingly writing the words for her grandchildren.

"You finished another copy of the Book of Commandments?" Alma asked as she sat in the seat across the table from Egyptus. "Who is this one for?"

"Levi and Lexa. They will marry soon." Egyptus sprinkled sand on the ink to absorb the moisture, then gently blew it off. "This is ready. I may make a basket for them from the papyrus, if we can get to it."

Alma nodded. "I should have known it would be for those two. Lexa will love it. They are waiting for the water to drain away so he can get something for their house ... I forgot what. The water is still high, nearly covering the papyrus plants. I cannot even get to the clay to make new pots yet."

"I suspect we will have to be patient and wait until the water drains away," Egyptus said, placing the lid on her ink and carefully setting her pens into the cup.

Kittens swatted and fought over a thread Egyptus had given them to play with. The kittens' eyes had opened, and they had grown enough to climb out of the basket and race around her home.

"Kittens!" Alma said, bending over to catch one with black mixed in with its yellow and set it in her lap. "Lexa would love one of these. I might, too. Let me ask Timor." The kitten curled up in her lap and slept. "These are so loving. Does their mama keep away the vermin?"

"I do not have any. Buttercup has always been good to keep mice, rats, and bugs out of my house," Egyptus said, glancing down to see if her cat lurked near the kittens. She sat under a chair, watching her kittens. "She is a good mama."

"The papyrus basket I made is light and strong," Alma said, rhythmically stroking the kitten and returning the conversation to papyrus and the receding flood water. "I overfilled a papyrus basket with squash and beans for a big meal I planned to serve to my mama and papa, Lexa, and Levi, and our children. I got more than I expected for the one small basket I carried with me."

"And it did not break?" Egyptus asked, widening her eyes. "Baskets cannot often hold that much."

"I know. It surprised me too. I expected I would need to set it down and empty half of it. I only got it home because Eber went with me to help carry it. The weight was too much for me."

"I do not think the baskets I made of hemp back in Shinar would have been able to carry so much without breaking. Perhaps a new one would, but they are heavy. I could not have carried it. Several heavy loads like the one you carried would have broken them. Did your basket show any wear?"

"None. I have carried heavy loads in it many times, and it still looks like I made it yesterday."

"Papyrus is an amazing plant," Egyptus said, shaking her head. "I never expected it to be strong. Because it is so light, I did not expect it to carry much weight."

"Not only that, but Eber wove a toy boat and took it out to the water —"

"In the floods? What about the wild animals swimming in the water?" Egyptus's voice lifted and she swallowed to control it. "Was he alone?"

"No. He took Kashet and Jov with him. They had swords with them in case an animal attacked, but none did."

"And the boat floated?"

Alma nodded.

"Made of papyrus?"

Alma nodded once more. "Yes. Eber wove it like he did other toys. He thought he would give it to one of his small cousins to play with, but he wanted to see if it would float first."

"And it did not sink?"

Alma shook her head. "He wove it tight so water would not get in. It amazed me to hear about the little boat floating." She traced the pattern of wood in Egyptus's table. "It made me wonder. Why can we not weave larger boats to get to the papyrus while the floods cover our land?"

"Do you have enough papyrus to make a boat large enough?"

"Not now, but we have some."

"How big would it have to be?"

Alma measured Egyptus's small kitchen with her eyes. "Perhaps as big or bigger than your table. Big enough for at least two to sit in. You would want at least one person with a sword to protect you from wild animals."

"It sounds like you have an idea that would help our community. What is keeping you from making the boat?" Egyptus asked. "You do not need my permission or Pharoah's, to try something new."

"You do not think the men would discredit my idea?"

"Why would they?"

"I have suggested other things. No one supported me."

"That will change," Egyptus said.

Alma set the sleeping kitten on her chair and stood. "I will have to think about it."

"Think about taking a kitten, too. It will need a home before too long."

"I am thinking of a kitten. I would like to be rid of the vermin."

Three days later, Egyptus climbed to the walkway on top of the wall as she did most days, hoping to see the floodwater gone. She leaned against the wall and gazed out. The water had receded enough she could finally see land between the bottom of the wall and the water.

As she watched, Eber, Kashet, and Jov ran out the gate with the little papyrus boat Alma had mentioned in her last visit. In their early teens, their laughter echoed up to the walkway, making them appear younger.

Kashet and Jov carried swords and watched diligently, searching for enemies, animal or human. When they reached the water's edge, Eber stooped and set the boat in.

Watching from the walkway at the top of the wall, Egyptus kept her eyes on the boys and the boat, hoping it would float. It dipped down, then lifted and danced on the waves, floating out away from the shore.

The boys bounced along the beach, following the small boat. Egyptus sucked in a breath, wondering if it would get away from them. It would be sad if they lost it.

Egyptus wanted to join the boys as they cheered the boat on as it bounced along the waves for many long breaths. Then a new wave caught it and pushed it toward the shore.

Eber raced down the shoreline to catch the boat before the waves pulled it out again. As he bent to retrieve his boat, a crocodile surged out of the water toward him.

Egyptus's heart leapt within her, beating wildly.

Kashet and Jov shouted and raced toward him with their swords, beating the crocodile over the head with their blades. Before the crocodile could snap his jaws over the boat and Eber's arm, he snatched his boat up and raced away.

As he ran, Eber fell backward, falling on one hand in the water. The crocodile surged toward the boy. Egyptus clung to the edge of the wall, fearing any sound she might make would give the crocodile an advantage. Jov caught Eber's hand and pulled him from the river, running with him out of the water and away from the crocodile.

The crocodile roared and slid back into the depths of the river. The three boys jumped up in celebration.

Egyptus fought to regain her breath after seeing the boys fight off the crocodile, cheering inside for the boys and their boat.

The three boys jogged toward the gate, laughing and cheering. Egyptus grinned with them. The boat had danced so prettily along the top of the waves. The boys would enjoy playing with it when the river's rushing flood waters receded, and it flowed with less force.

Alma moved from the other end of the walkway where she had been watching the boys to stand next to Egyptus. "Did you see Eber?"

"That boat nearly got your son's arm taken off by that crocodile!"

"Yes, I know. I could not breathe while they fought the beast." She clutched her dress near her heart until her excitement overcame the past fears. "But did you see the boat skip along the waves?"

"It was beautiful to see."

"If he makes one that floats that well and big enough for people to ride on, we can get to the papyrus plants easier. Do you see it going out on the Siddim Sea?"

"That would be interesting," Alma said, nodding thoughtfully. "But I believe if we can travel on the river in boats, we should be able to ride out on the Siddim."

"Not on those little ones?" Egyptus said with a little gasp.

"No, but bigger boats could carry us."

"Where would we travel on them? What would they do?" Egyptus asked, drawing her eyebrows together. Travel could be dangerous, especially since others had moved through their land. Could they travel without being attacked? Would it be easier and safer than their travel from the plains of Shinar?

"From here to there, to the different parts of land separated by water. Perhaps we could even sail up the river —"

"Up the river?" Egyptus gulped. "Past the waterfall?"

"We could carry the boat on the land around the falls. But we could trade with others who live along the river."

"Others? You expect to find others to trade with us after the attacks we have suffered from them?"

Alma shrugged. "Someday they will forget their anger and hatred and will want to trade for things we have. It may not be this year —"

"Or next year!" Egyptus exclaimed.

"It may not be for many years. By then, we will have learned how to direct our boats where we want them to go, rather than trust the waves and the water to carry them."

"What do you think it will take to control them?" Egyptus's interest in the idea grew as they spoke. She could imagine riding in a boat like the little one, but larger, out to the big islands of papyrus, floating down to the Siddim for salt or fishing. All would be easier riding in a boat. She leaned on the wall and watched others venture past the gate.

Alma grimaced. "I do not know. But we have the time to figure it out. I trust Jehovah to help me and the boys create a solution."

"Good for you, Alma. You and the boys are creative. How long did it take to weave the bigger boat?"

"Eber and I worked together on it since before we talked about it. We tried it out in the wash pot to be sure it would float before taking it to the river."

"Smart. You did well. That boat danced on the water."

Alma grinned. "Thank you. But the hard work begins now as we enlarge it. I think we must do it slowly to ensure we do not lose the grace and style of the boat."

"You would not want to lose its ability to float, either," Egyptus agreed. "If there is anything I can do to help ..."

"We will come to you, Mama Egypt. Thank you for offering. You always have wonderful ideas of ways to solve our problems."

Egyptus pushed herself away from the wall and brushed the dust from the front of her dress. "I have the blessing of having read all the books the matriarchs wrote. I learned much from Eve."

"You read Eve's book?" Alma asked with a weak, pensive smile.

Egyptus nodded.

"I forgot your mama had copies of all those books. You *were* blessed. It is too bad you did not bring them with you."

"I would have brought them if they were mine. But they were not. They belong to my mama and I left them with her in Shinar. I am certain she took them with her when they left." Egyptus sighed. "It would be lovely to read from them again. I miss my old friends."

"I never saw them," Alma said, brushing her hair back. "My mama did not have her own copy."

"Few women did. Mama met with Grandpapa Methuselah before he died. All the other matriarchs had died except Noah's wife, Grandmama Imma. She already had her own copies. Many came directly from the matriarchs, so Grandpapa Methuselah gave his wife's books to Mama."

"That must have been before the flood?"

"It was. Mama's books were her most prized possessions, them and her healing salves and concoctions. She insisted on bringing them on the ark with her."

"You are blessed to have Ham and Basya as your parents. Most of us here," Alma spread her arms wide to include the village of Egypt, "are many generations from Grandpapa Noah and Grandmama Imma. I hardly knew them before we left Shinar."

"I was blessed to be Basya's and Ham's youngest child."

Alma invited Egyptus to join her family each time Eber, Jov, Kashet, and Alma created and tested a new boat. They continued to use Alma's large washing pot to see if it would float before taking it to the river for a test on the waves.

During that time, the flood waters finally receded and the Black River slowed, no longer racing past the village. When they took the trial boats to it, they no longer had to struggle against rogue waves dragging the boat beneath the water, although they kept a vigilant guard against crocodiles. Sometimes the boat slipped under the water. Most other times, it floated on top. Egyptus offered suggestions when asked and celebrated with Alma and the young men when the boat floated.

In time, the land dried sufficiently, and the boys were called to join the men to plant the fields. Although the ground still muddied their feet, they stepped across it side by side, as in years before to scatter seeds across the ground. After working with their papas in the fields all day, the boys spent evenings weaving and adjusting the boat.

One day, about four weeks after the first toy boat bounced on the waves of the flooding Black River, Lexa tapped on Egyptus's open door.

"Does your mama have a new trial of the boat for us to test?" Egyptus asked as the young woman entered.

"She will by tomorrow, but that is not why I came to visit today. Levi will have our home ready for us before I am ready to move in. Mama is busy. Can you help me finish my dress and some of the other things I need for our home?"

Egyptus leapt from her chair and hugged her granddaughter. "You know I would love to help you. What can I do?"

Lexa set down her basket and lifted a kitten from a seat and sat in it across from her grandmama, holding the kitten in her lap and petting it.

"This kitten is lovely. I would ... No. I am here for other help. I do not know what gifts others will give us, but there is so much we will need. I am overwhelmed and have little time." Lexa nearly cried in frustration.

Egyptus remembered her own frustration in the days before she married Afra. "Tell me what you have."

Lexa set the kitten beside her before opening the basket she brought with her. "I need help with finishing my dress. Can we work on it while we talk?"

Egyptus agreed, then retrieved her needles. They sat together stitching the hem of the dress and talking about the items Lexa would absolutely need for her new home.

"You will need towels."

"I have them. I made towels first when I learned to weave."

Egyptus nodded. "Blankets?"

"I wove those earlier too."

"Those are important. What about dishes for eating and pots for cooking?"

"Mama had me make those early while she taught me to make pots and dishes."

"Excellent. Those are the most important things to have." Egyptus crunched her eyebrows together in thought. "Do you have pillows for your bed?"

"I do."

They went through a list of other required home-making items Lexa would need in her new home. She had already made most of the things she needed as a young girl. Alma had prepared her well.

"What would you like me to do to help prepare for your new home?" Egyptus asked at last.

"I may need more pots?"

"You will probably receive some at your marriage celebration."

"I have candles."

"That is good. We need fat from the animals for candles."

"I know," Lexa said. "I want something special to give to Levi. What can I give to him?"

Egyptus rested a finger near her mouth as she thought. "Perhaps you can make him a new tunic to wear for the wedding rite?"

The kitten that had slept peacefully next to Lexa woke, stretched, and jumped off the seat.

"He is a beauty," Lexa hummed, watching him strut across the floor to the kitchen and food.

"He is a nice cat, but all of Buttercup's kittens are nice. He is almost old enough to leave his mama. Would you like him?"

Lexa's head jerked up. "A kitten would be nice to have in our new home."

"They keep your home free of vermin. He is here for you if you and Levi decide you want him."

"I may. Thank you. Levi's mama is making him a new tunic, but I want to give him a new tunic as well."

"He would like that. Do you need my help?"

Lexa set her hands on the dress on her lap. "If you will add a flower design to the waist of my dress, I will have time to make Levi's tunic."

"I can do that. What flower design would you like? In what color?"

"I would like bluebells. Can you sew little bluebells around the waist of my dress?" Lexa bit her lower lip. "You have done so much for me. I hate to ask."

"I can do that. Your hem is in." Egyptus left to find some blue and green thread for sewing the flowers. Lexa had pulled the pieces for the tunic from her basket and began stitching the seams when Egyptus returned with the thread.

The two women worked side by side until the sun dropped low in the sky.

"Oh!" Lexa exclaimed, dropping the tunic to the floor. "I am expected to join Levi and his family for dinner. I must leave."

Egyptus allowed a gentle smile to fill her face. "You should leave then. You do not want to miss dinner with Tama and Shiblom. She is an excellent cook."

Lexa grinned back at Egyptus. "She is. She has helped me improve my cooking. I must go." She gathered up her sewing, kissed Egyptus on the cheek, and rushed from the house.

Egyptus stood and stretched, thinking to light candles and continue working on the dress, but Ami knocked on the door.

"Mama wants you to come to dinner. She saw you working with Lexa and knows you have not prepared a meal for yourself," Ami said. "Besides, I miss having you visit us."

Egyptus gave Ami a quick hug, then looked behind her for Adok and Rivka, who usually followed her everywhere. "Where are your shadows?"

"Mama gave them chores to do so I could come alone to get you for dinner."

"I appreciate that. I miss our visits as well." Egyptus checked her fire before joining Ami at her door. "How is your writing coming? Do you still write stories?" Egyptus asked as she closed her door and walked together across the space between their homes.

"I try to write in the short time alone I get each day. I am writing a story about wandering through the wilderness to get here. I remember the days we were so hungry."

Egyptus shuddered. "I remember those days too. We were so hungry. I did not think we would survive to find our new home."

"I knew we would. I prayed to Jehovah. A quiet voice whispered to me, telling me we would find food and survive."

"I did not know that," Egyptus said. She took Ami's hand and squeezed it.

"I do not share with many that it happened. It is sacred to me." Ami opened the door to her mama's kitchen and held it open for her grandmama.

"As it should be," Egyptus said as she entered the kitchen. She inhaled the fragrance of the cooking meal and smiled. "Thank you for inviting me, Xenia."

Xenia looked up from her cooking fire. "I knew you should come for dinner. I saw you were busy with Lexa all afternoon."

"She asked me to help with her dress. They will celebrate their wedding rite soon."

Pharoah entered the kitchen. "Levi asked to visit with me after our evening meal. They will probably ask for a time for that rite."

Egyptus nodded. "When will you have time for it?"

"We will have all the seeds planted soon. It will not be long before we have other things to do with our days. I suspect they will want me to perform the rite soon."

"I expect they will," Xenia said. "They will want time together before they are called on to join with the community when we go to the Siddim Sea to gather salt." She turned to Ami. "Go help your brother and sister wash for dinner. I sent them out already."

Ami hurried outside to find her brother and sister.

"It will not be long before we set a time for Ami's wedding rite," Xenia said.

Egyptus gasped. "She is too young still."

"For now, but it will not be long."

New Lives

L exa hurried into Egyptus's home with a cry and bouncing on her toes the next morning. "I must finish this tunic. Pharoah will perform the wedding rite for Levi and me on the Fifth Day next week. That is only nine days away."

"You are nearly ready," Egyptus said. "We went through all the things you need yesterday"

"There are a few things —"

"There are always things you would like to have, but you can make them later. You are ready."

"Except for this tunic and my dress." Lexa nodded toward her dress that Egyptus had laid on the back of the seat. "I see you have been working on it."

"I spent some time on it last night, some this morning."

Lexa sat in the seat across from Egyptus and pulled the tunic for Levi from her basket. "I have not had time to work more on this last night or this morning. It is good to come over here to work. No one interrupts me."

Egyptus grinned, remembering the days her family interrupted her preparations for her own marriage. She pulled the dress onto her lap and found her needle. One of the yellow kittens leapt on the seat beside her and crawled onto her lap beneath the dress, curling up and quickly falling asleep. Egyptus stroked its soft fur a few times before picking up the needle and stabbing it through the fabric. "Family is like that. They always have something to say or something for you to do."

Lexa found her needle and stabbed it into the seam. "Another kitten. That one is beautiful." She poked her needle in and out along the seam for a few breaths. "I cannot believe how many silly little things my brothers find for me to do."

"Your brothers want you to know they will miss you. It is difficult to have a sister leave and make a home of her own."

Lexa's needle slid in and out, closing the seam. "I know they will miss me. I missed Alma when she married Timor, even though she did not move far from our home. The home Levi is building for me is close to Mama and Papa, but my brothers act like I will leave for the other side of the world."

Buttercup walked into the sitting room from Egyptus's bedroom. The other kittens followed behind, tumbling over one another.

Egyptus giggled. "Like kittens, brothers are funny. Mine did many of the same things, although I moved to the far end of the valley, far away from our home."

"You never talk about those days," Lexa said, grabbing up a kitten and petting it.

"It was long ago, and I miss my Afra. It makes me sad to remember those days."

"You should write the story of your love for your children and grand-children to read. I know I would like to read it." The kitten kneaded

Lexa's skirt with its paws, then snuggled into her lap and fell asleep. She returned to sending her needle speeding through the seam.

Would writing the story of joining Afra as his bride bring him closer to me or cause me to weep because he is gone?

Egyptus lifted a shoulder in a small shrug. "I may do that. I suppose you girls should know how I came to be Afra's wife. He was the love of my life."

The kitten in Egyptus's lap woke and stretched before jumping down to play with the other kittens.

Through the morning as they worked, Egyptus shared snippets of stories about her youth and how she and Afra had become husband and wife. She found sharing brought her joy, although she shed more than a few tears remembering those days. The kitten in Lexa's lap woke and jumped down, stalking away in search of his mama and litter mates.

Egyptus grinned at the kitten. "Perhaps I will write that story for you and the other girls after all."

"And the men. They will want to know about the love you and Grandpapa Afra had."

"Perhaps. I have not seen men as interested in those stories."

"I suspect it is because you have not shared yours with them. My brothers like to hear Papa tell about how he and Mama found each other and the stories of their courtship."

"Perhaps it would be different if that lioness had not attacked Afra ..." Egyptus sighed. "I miss my Afra. However, I have learned that Jehovah needs him to be where he is. I want him to be here with me always, but I will survive."

"Will you marry again?"

Egyptus glanced up sharply. "Who would I marry? There are no men in Egypt my age who are not already married. And I do not want another woman's man, or any other man. I am happy to be alone."

"I had not thought about the who. We younger women have choices of the young men. You have no one. I am sorry." Lexa slid from her seat and hugged Egyptus.

"I am happy here with my children and grandchildren. You all make me happy, you and those like your parents who came with us across the wilderness to find this land. You bring me joy."

"A liquid joy, sometimes," Lexa said, pulling her linen cloth from her pocket and wiping away Egyptus's tears. "Your tears make your story special," she said, moving back to her chair.

Egyptus wiped away the last of her tears and pulled the needle through the dress, then tied off the last stitch. "There. I finished your dress. You will look beautiful in it."

Lexa held up the tunic she had been stitching. "And I have completed Levi's tunic. Thank you for sharing your time with me. I could never have finished this at home on my own."

When Lexa left with her dress and the tunic she had made for Levi, Egyptus retrieved the scroll containing the Book of Commandments she had copied for them. She scanned through it, checking for errors and smudges. Finding none, she carefully set it inside a large pot she had made during the last warm days for the next couple to marry. She would give these to the young couple at the wedding celebration.

Perhaps a kitten would be ready to leave Buttercup as well.

Between helping Alma and the young men test their new boat and help-ing her granddaughters with their children, Egypt stayed busy during the next week leading up to Lexa's and Levi's marriage celebration. She thanked Jehovah many times that she had completed her gift for them early, for she would not have had the time to finish it in those last two weeks and still help her family.

She sat in her favorite place in the sanctuary the morning of the wedding rite, enjoying the sounds of appreciation and the whispered comments about the sewing she had done on the dress from the women who sat near her. The modest dress looked lovely on Lexa. She was a beautiful bride.

After the rite, Lexa and Levi were surprised to receive a copy of the Book of Commandments. "I thought we missed out since you gave all the families a copy of this earlier," Levi said.

"We will need this," Lexa said. "We need to remember the covenants and commandments Jehovah gave us."

"I believe every family should have easy access to these," Egypt said. "How can we obey commandments we do not know?"

"It is not possible," Levi said.

"I love the pot too," Lexa said. "When did you make this?"

"Last year. I knew you two would marry sometime. I made several so I would have them available to give when the next couples married."

"Great plan," Lexa said, kissing Egypt on the cheek.

Later, while people ate and visited, Isa sat beside Egypt at a table. "I heard you helped Lexa with her dress. It is beautiful."

"It helps that she is a beautiful young woman," Egyptus said, allowing her lips to curve into a smile. "She did most of the work. The style she chose flatters her."

"It does that," Isa said as she watched the young couple.

"How are your healing plants surviving?" Egyptus asked.

"They would do better if I could leave them in the same soil all the time. It does not help them to dig them up and move them when the floods come."

"What can we do about that?" Egyptus leaned her elbows on the table.

"I wish I knew. There has to be a way to protect them. A wall does not help, as we saw this year. Besides, a wall would shade my plants from the sun. I wish we could move onto our land and not worry about floods and enemies."

"I am certain that would make your life easier," Egyptus said. "There has to be a way to do that. We must think about it more and solve this problem. It will make our people happier to have more space and to live without being so close. Jehovah warned us we would be happier if we have more space between us."

"But the floods and our enemies have made that impossible." Isa leaned her head on her hand.

"We will find a way to solve these problems."

Pym hurried to where Egyptus and Isa sat visiting and skidded to a stop. "We need your help, Isa. Rebecca is having ..." He stopped to catch his breath.

"It is her time?" Egyptus asked.

Pym nodded. "Help."

"Take her home. Carry her if you must. I will go get my basket of healing supplies and meet you there," Isa said.

"I will come with you, Pym," Egyptus said. "You may need help to get Rebecca home."

Egyptus and Isa stepped out of Pym's and Rebecca's home as the sun rose the next morning. They took a deep breath of the cool early morning air.

"That went easier than I expected," Egyptus said.

"Why?" Isa asked. "Rebecca is young and healthy. All babies should come as easily as their little Aliyah. She is a beauty."

Egyptus stretched and yawned. "She is. She looks much like her mama did. Rebecca is special to me."

"Last children are always special, as are the first. Rebecca will remember this day." Isa covered a yawn. "These late nights are not as easy as they were when we were young."

"You are not old," Egyptus said. "I am still older than you. Do you remember your first child's birth?" She stepped off the porch and walked toward the path leading to her home.

Isa walked beside her. "I always will. Yehoram was in a hurry to live a mortal life. His birth is one of the easiest my mama helped with. He changed as he aged. By the time we considered coming with you, and the others of our family who had joined yours, Nimrod had blinded Yehoram."

"I almost forgot about Yehoram," Egyptus said, sadness engulfing her. "He did not come often to visit with you when you came to visit Afra and me."

"No." Isa allowed a sigh to slip from deep within her and gazed off to the northwest as if she were hoping to see him cross the wilderness. "He joined Nimrod early on his hunting trips and came to believe himself to be a greater hunter than Nimrod himself. He watched the building of the tower with great interest, joining in often to add bricks to the walls."

"It is sorrowful to leave children behind. I will always miss Shim and his family. But Abigail would not leave her mama. I often wonder what happened to his family."

"You do not dream of them as you have dreamed of your mama and papa?" Isa asked, stopping at the place where the paths crossed.

"No. I have not dreamed of Shim since we left Shinar. It is strange. I thought I would when I dreamed of the great divide, but I never saw Shim. I do not know what happened to him and his family."

"Losing our children is difficult," Isa said. "I can only hope our sons found as good of a place to make a home as we did."

"It is all we can hope for," Egyptus said. She embraced her friend and strode the rest of the way to her little home.

Buttercup met her at the door, mewling for food and water. Egyptus found small scraps of meat to share with the cat and the kittens left in her home, filled a bowl with fresh water, then found her way to bed.

Alma had already taken one of the yellow kittens to her home. Egyptus planned to take one of the black and yellow kittens to Lexa and Levi in a few days after they had time to be alone for a while.

Sometime later, she turned over, only to find a warm body beside her feet. "Thank you, Buttercup," she mumbled, and fell back to sleep.

That afternoon, she visited the new baby. Rebecca and Pym had slept most of the day, only waking to care for little Aliyah's needs. Egyptus went to the cooking fire and heated a meal for them.

Each morning for a week, she slipped into Rebecca's kitchen to prepare food for the young couple. Then one morning, she stepped into the kitchen to discover Rebecca preparing grains for herself and Pym.

"I can cook for us now," Rebecca said. "Thank you for all you have done for us, but I am stronger now and can cook for my family."

Egyptus gazed down into the basket holding little Aliyah. "I see you are prepared for this." She touched the baby's cheek, then turned. "I can make my morning meal at home. Enjoy your little family."

Rebecca has become a mama. She no longer needs me for now. That will change as it has with others. She sighed. *I hoped it would last a bit longer, but now I can sleep longer.*

Experiments

O ver the next days, Egypt pondered on the problem of spreading out safely as she worked to plant her garden. They would have to solve the flooding problem and resolve the need to protect each family without keeping them within the close walls of Egypt.

As the people moved apart into their own lands and settled into families again, the women would be less willing to have their men march out to battle other villages. She hoped that time would help to solve that problem.

That was only one problem, and with Jehovah's help, they would resolve it in time. The other problem, however, was more difficult to solve. They did not control the river. But they could, Egypt was certain. She had to think about it for a time, with the help of others.

She feared Gilit would cause problems with these solutions. She so often found reasons to complain. She prayed often to have compassion for the lonely woman, whose only companion through the day was her dog. But she had a husband.

As she worked copying the Book of Commandments for other young couples and other chores, she returned to her concern about controlling the river. There had to be a way to control it, or Jehovah would not have sent them to this land.

A wall had stopped the water from entering their village. Could they direct the flood with a sort of wall? What would work?

Amid all her pondering, Alma invited Egyptus to join them to test their latest version of their ship. The floods had receded enough for them to find quiet pools of water along the banks of the river.

Eber brought his friends, Kashet and Jov, to fight off any wild creatures that might seek to attack them. They held their swords ready and stared into the river before nodding, giving Alma and Egyptus permission to set the larger boat into the quiet pool.

Alma set it in the water and gave it a gentle nudge. The boat floated out into the pool.

Egyptus watched the boat float, hoping it would stay on the surface. It floated out into the center of the pool.

A breeze caught the boat, pushing it out further. It wobbled on the little wave, then righted itself. Egyptus let out the breath she held. The boys cheered.

She glanced down into the water in time to see a shadow slide beneath the boat. "Look out! Something is —"

The creature in the water swam up, bumping into the bottom of the little boat. The boat stuttered in the water before tipping over and slowly sinking.

Eber started to wade out into the water, but Jov grabbed him by the back of his tunic. "The boat is not worth going into the water. Did you not see what tipped over our boat?"

A chill rushed through Egyptus.

"No. I was watching the boat float. What tipped it over?" Eber asked, stepping back onto the riverbank.

"A small crocodile swam beneath the boat. You do not want to encounter a crocodile in the water, big or little."

Egyptus shivered.

"Stay out of the water!" Alma screamed, pointing at the surfacing crocodile.

Eber ran backward, stumbling over a rock and falling. Jov helped him up and they stepped back quickly, away from the river. Egyptus and Alma followed, with Kashet coming at the back with his sword raised, watching for the crocodile to come out of the water.

When they were far enough away, they stopped and turned toward the river.

"It floated!" Eber whooped.

"Until the crocodile tipped it over," Kashet said.

"We need something that will not tip over so easily," Jov said.

"We can do hard things," Eber said.

"Back to work," Jov said, turning to walk back toward the village wall.

"Yes. Back to work. At least we know it still floats. Now we need to make it big enough to ride in and sturdy enough a crocodile cannot tip it over."

"Those are two sizeable challenges," Egyptus said, following the boys and enjoying their excitement.

"We can do it," Eber said. "Our earlier trials worked. We can fix this problem, too."

Egyptus grinned.

"We need to make it —" Jov said as the young men started running through the gate.

"I love the enthusiasm these boys have," Alma said.

"They are intelligent and optimistic boys. They will solve these problems and any others that come up," Egyptus said, closing the gate behind them. "No need to let wild animals in."

"What will you do when they finish their boat?" she asked Alma.

"After they learn to control it and go where we want? Float down the river and explore, then come back up again. Maybe discover ways to get from here to there faster."

Egyptus nodded. "It will be good to travel across the valley in a boat."

"I agree. That was my idea. Or, if I am honest, it was Eber's idea, along with Jov and Kashet."

"I like the way you and your family think."

"We are your grandchildren."

"We can do hard things," Egyptus said, mimicking Eber.

The earth dried and the Black River slowed, growing smaller as the sun heated the land. Egyptus joined some of her family camping in the cool of the hills.

Sitting in the shade of the tall trees with her grandchildren, she watched them play near the creek that flowed past their camp.

"Grandmama," Chayim's and Cira's little three-year-old son, Aker, said. "Play with me."

Egyptus scooted close to see what he did as he played. He dug along the edge of the water in the mud. "What are you doing? Are you trying to dig clay?"

"No, Grandmama," he said. "I am digging a river to water my plants. See?" He pointed at the tiny flowers he had poked into the ground a distance from the creek. He dragged a finger through the dirt between the creek and his little plants.

"That should help get water to them," she said.

"Yes," he crowed. "Help me."

Egyptus picked up a little stick and began digging from the creek toward the little plants. Water seeped into the little river, soaking into the dirt before filling. Aker and Egyptus scraped their sticks ahead of the water, encouraging it to flow until it reached the flowers, soaking them.

"I remember reading a story when Eve and Adam did this to water their fields," Egyptus said.

"Did they dig little rivers to get the water from the river?" Aker asked.

"They did, especially when the rains stopped falling."

"The rains stop here. We should dig little rivers to our fields," Aker said in a solemn voice sounding identical to his papa.

Soon the water rushed down the little rivulet, flooding the little flowers and threatening to wash them away.

"Make it stop, Grandmama!" Aker cried.

Egyptus dug a little canal back toward the creek, encouraging the water to flow away from the flowers. Soon only a trickle of water continued to drip toward the little plants.

"That is one way to control the water," Egyptus mused. "There must be other ways."

She filled the space at the beginning of the little river with dirt until the water stopped flowing. They dug more rivulets and dammed them many times before Cira called them to dinner and they left their play.

"Grandmama! You let him get muddy?" Cira cried, then stared at Egyptus, who also had muddy hands. "You two need to go back and wash your hands."

Egyptus glanced at her hands, then the little boy's hands, shaking her head. "Aker, we need to clean this mud from our hands before we eat. Your mama's good food will not taste as nice if we eat with muddy hands." She caught the little boy by the hand and hurried back to the stream before he could complain. "We get to play in the water a bit longer," she whispered.

The boy's near whimper became soft giggles as they knelt next to the stream and washed the mud from their hands.

"Can we do this again?" Aker asked.

"I would like that," Egyptus said. "Perhaps tomorrow."

I want to see if I can discover a way to control the floods.

Aker grabbed her hand and walked with her back to the campfire where his mama waited for them. He held up his hands. "No more mud, Mama."

Cira inspected his hands. "You and Grandmama did well. Are you hungry?"

**

Every day during the week while they camped, Egyptus and the children played in the mud building wider streams flowing away from the creek. Each time, she tried to direct the water away from the tiny houses the children had built. Sometimes the floods washed away the houses. The little children cried until Egyptus suggested they could do something to stop the water from flooding their homes.

Aker and his friends built a wall of sticks around their village, trying to protect it. "Like daddy built around our village," Aker said.

Sometimes the wall worked. Other times it did not. If the children built their village on a hill, the water stayed out. If they did not, their houses flooded.

Then Egyptus tried something new to control the flooding water. She scraped a long line of soil, tamping it down so it would not wash away. She wanted to see if the wall of soil would divert the floods.

When the children sent flood waters down a small river near it, she watched to see what would happen. The water eroded the long hill along the edges where they had not tamped it down hard enough, but the water raced around the areas where they had tightly packed the dirt. It passed the barrier, not damaging anything on the other side.

Egyptus and the children cheered.

They spent many hours together, trying other ways to slow down or stop the floods while they camped in the hills. Some worked. Others did not work as well.

When Egyptus returned to her little home, she recorded the results of her experiments with controlling flood waters in her journal.

She sighed as she closed her journal. The big problem remained. How could she transfer the things she learned with the children to protecting their homes from the Black River?

The morning after returning home, Egyptus stepped out her door to pick vegetables for her dinner. As she stared at the garden, she gasped. It required much attention.

Not even gentle rains had fallen in the time she hid from the heat in the mountains. Although she had asked Adok to water her plants while she was gone, the plants drooped and the ground around them had hardened.

She groaned, thinking about work required to carry water to her vegetables. She found a bucket and took it to the well. If she expected her plants to live, they needed water.

"I am sorry, Grandmama," Adok cried when he saw his grandmama toting water from the well to her garden. "Papa kept me busy working in the fields every day. I promised myself I would wake up early to water your garden, but I was exhausted." The boy toed the hard ground. "I did not remember until later in the day." Tears leaked from his eyes.

Egyptus set her buckets down and drew him into an embrace. "I think my garden will survive. Look, the plants are already lifting their heads to the sun. Do you have time to help me now?"

Adok glanced around. "I think I have finished everything Papa wanted me to do for now. How can I help?" A little smile brightened his face.

Egyptus grinned. "Get another bucket and help me carry water."

Adok turned to race to the little building that held garden tools, returning with a bucket banging against the back of his legs.

Egyptus had drizzled water from her bucket over her plants, emptying it. She walked to the well with Adok. He pulled on the rope that brought the bucket of water up. He poured it first into her bucket, then into his. They walked back along the path toward her home and garden together, careful not to spill any water.

At the garden, Adok carefully poured a little stream of water over the dry plants while Egyptus spilled water over plants in another part of the garden.

Soon the buckets were empty. They walked back to the well and refilled them. Three trips later, all the plants had received water and were now lifting their heads to the sun.

"I should have done this differently," Egyptus said with a start.

"How could you have?" Adok asked.

"I have been trying to teach myself how to control the river. We could have made little lengths of river through the plants and poured water into the ends. The water would have run down the rivulets to the plants with less work."

"Next time," Adok said. "I will help you dig the rivers tomorrow, when the ground between your plants has dried some."

Egyptus nodded at her young grandson. "That will work. Tomorrow is the Sabbath, but we can work on it again the next day."

She considered the project with some excitement. The rivulets between the plants would be larger than the little bits of tiny river she and the grandchildren had dug in the hills. She could see if the things she tried would work on a bigger scale.

Early on the day after the Sabbath, Adok knocked at Egyptus's door. "I am ready to help," he said.

"Help?" Her face wrinkled as she tried to remember what he was there to help with.

"With your little rivers in your garden."

"Oh. I almost forgot." Egyptus set the dish she had washed on the table and dried her hands on a towel. "I am ready. What can we use to dig those?"

"I have been thinking about how we can dig them," Adok said as he grabbed her hand. "I think Papa has something in the gardening building."

He swung her hand back and forth as they walked to look for a tool. "Papa uses a tool much like your staff when we plant melons. It stabs a hole in the dirt to make a hole for the little plants."

"I remember that tool," Egyptus said. It had a sharpened end. "Do you think it will work to make the rivers?"

"I think it will. We should try them."

Egyptus considered the suggestion as they walked together to the building. She had helped her papa plant corn and other vegetables that way. She should have remembered the tool.

They retrieved two of the sharpened sticks from the tool building and returned to her garden. The plants were wilting already.

"We should dig your rivers quickly, Grandmama, so your plants do not dry out," Adok said.

They worked together to drag the sticks between the plants. The baking hot sun had dried the soil hard and heavy, making it difficult to dig the little rivulets.

"I will go get some water," Adok said, dropping his digging stick. "It is easier to dig in wet dirt."

He hurried away to get a bucket and fill it with water before Egyptus could ask about it. She grinned at his retreating back before stabbing the stick in the ground and dragging it between the wilting vegetables.

She had made a little progress when Adok returned with his bucket filled with water. He gently dripped water into her shallow furrow. Egyptus allowed the moisture to soak in before dragging her stick along its length to deepen it.

Working as a team, Adok dripped water and Egyptus dug deeper troughs. After a span, they had more than half the furrows dug between the plants.

Egyptus stood and stretched her back as she surveyed the remainder of her garden.

"If you pour the water, I will dig," Adok suggested.

Egyptus gazed at the boy. "This is harder work than I expected. But you are correct. We should trade tasks."

Sighing deeply, she bent to lift the full bucket of water Adok left sitting at the top of the next row of plants. Her back twinged in complaint, but she ignored it as she poured a small stream of water a short distance between the plants. The fresh fragrance of muddy soil wafted through the air.

The water soaked in and Adok scraped a new furrow in the softened dirt. They worked together another half span, trading places once more when Adok ran to get another bucket of water.

Egyptus stood among her garden plants when Adok returned. He stumbled on a rock, splashing water on her feet and on the plants.

"Oh, no!" he cried. "I am sorry to soak your feet like that."

"Do not concern yourself with my wet feet," Egyptus said. "The water cools them. Look. The water flows down our rivers, giving water to the plants."

Water spread out, filling the rivulets and beneath the plants, even the ones without furrows dug between them.

Adok grabbed his digging stick and joined Egyptus hastily scraping rivers between the last rows of vegetables. Soon all the rows had little rivulets dug between them.

Egyptus leaned on her digging stick as she waited for Adok to return with another bucket of water. He carefully poured water into the top of each little furrow. After two more buckets of water, all the plants were standing straight, drinking in the moisture through their roots and stretching up to absorb the sunlight.

"I will bring more water tomorrow, Grandmama," Adok promised.

"If your papa gives you time," Egyptus said with a grin.

That evening, as she considered the need to control the floods and the little rivulets between her rows of plants, a gentle breeze caressed her face.

She closed her eyes. *'Is it you, Afra? Am I thinking correctly? Will this help solve the bigger problem?'*

'You are making progress. Soon you will have learned enough to help Egypt. Keep working. You will get it.'

'I miss you. You could solve this problem so much faster than me.'

'You know it is your problem to solve. Father needs me here. You will solve it.'

The breeze caressed her face once more before leaving through the open door.

Tears leaked from her eyes. She loved Afra's visits, but she missed him so. She wanted to feel his arms around her once more.

Hard Things

Adok returned each morning with buckets of water for Egyptus's garden. After the first morning, she allowed him to water her garden without supervision while she worked on other projects outside the house. Sometimes that happened to be helping Alma and the boys with their boat.

The past three times they took the new boats to the river, the larger boats sank. Sadly, the boys carried their drowned boat between them back to the village, glumly discussing the problems that may have caused the boat to sink rather than dance over the water.

"They are not overly concerned about their failures," Egyptus said to Alma as they trailed the boys back to the village. "I expected them to be more upset."

"We discussed the challenges of learning new things," Alma explained. "We talked about how building a new boat is like that. Each failure teaches them something new. They will solve the problems sooner than they expect."

"Probably before I resolve the problem of our flooding river. We need the flood water to help keep the fields fertile, but we do not want it to flood our homes and other lands."

"You will find the answer," Alma said, patting Egyptus on the shoulder. "You can do hard things as well as the boys. You are working on the problem like the boys are. I hope you discover a solution soon. We need our homes to be safer. The wall helps, but when the floods are high like they were this year, even the wall cannot keep the water out."

The women opened the gate and entered the village. Alma pulled it closed behind them. "We do not want any creatures following us inside when no one is watching."

"Especially those serpents," Egyptus agreed.

"We do not need the hippopotamuses to come in either. They are too big for our little community. Imagine the damage they would cause."

Egyptus nodded and gazed across the gate. A hippopotamus lumbered toward the wall. She shuddered and pointed at him. "He could cause some humongous damage."

They dropped the locking log into place across the gate.

"He could. We need to be certain the gate locks. It is good the men reinforced the walls after the rains stopped, fixing it so the serpents cannot slither through," Alma said.

Egyptus shivered. Pharoah had insisted that the men strengthen the gate and walls after the recent rains weakened them. The hippopotamus bumped into the gate, causing it to shake.

The women yelped and stared at the gate. Egyptus silently prayed it would hold against the weight of the enormous animal.

When the gate did not give way or open, the giant beast lumbered away. Egyptus and Alma expelled an extra-large sigh. Egyptus glanced at Alma and giggled.

"Good thing the men strengthened that gate. If we could solve all our other problems —"

"We will. The boys are intelligent. They will soon have another boat ready to test."

"And you will discover a way to control that river."

"The river is necessary, but we need to keep the floods from ruining our homes," Egyptus said as they turned from the gate and walked into the village.

"It would be nice to occupy the land we claimed when we first arrived here in Egypt," Alma said. "I love living here with everyone else, but it would be nice to live on and use our land."

"You are not the only one who wants to move into the valley. If we can control the river ..."

"The river and the enemies. Now that the river will not flood until next year and the big cats have moved on ..."

"Do not say it, Alma. We enjoy our peace."

"I do as well, Mama Egyptus," Alma said quickly. "But we both know Ludim and the others will return."

"I hope we frightened them off when we took them into the wilderness."

"And when the big cats chose to help protect us. But Ludim and his men will return. They will see the cats are gone and we have no extra defense."

"I know. I hope they wait a long time before they return," Egyptus said. "However, that is no reason to stop practicing with our staffs. We cannot depend soley on hope. We must always be prepared."

"I agree, Mama Egyptus, although it is sometimes difficult to crawl out of my warm bed early in the morning."

The women stopped next to the well. Egyptus dropped the bucket into the well and pulled it back to the top. "It is always difficult to leave my warm bed in the morning," she said, dipping the dipper that hung on the side of the well into the bucket and handing it to Alma to drink. "We do it because we must. I do not want to be taken as prisoner by Ludim or any other man."

"Do you ever want to find another man?" Alma said as she handed the dipper back to Egyptus.

Egyptus stared at the daughter of her heart for a long breath before shaking off the hurt. "No. I miss Afra too much to desire another man." *Besides, he still comes to visit me.*

"And who would ... Who could take his place?" Egyptus continued. "No one. Definitely not the boy, Ludim. I cared for him as a child. I have no desire for him or any other man except my Afra."

"You are so alone," Alma argued.

"But not lonely. I have you and my other children and grandchildren and my friends here in Egypt to keep me company." She patted Alma's cheek. "Do not worry about me. I am happy waiting to join Afra."

"Not soon," Alma protested.

"No. Not soon, nor soon enough. I will join him when Jehovah determines I have lived long enough."

"I pray that does not happen for a long time," Alma said.

As the villagers harvested the grains at the end of the warm season and prepared to winnow the chaff, Cira doubled over with her hands clamped on her stomach. "My baby is coming," she cried.

Isa and Chayim left the others to finish caring for the grains, helping Cira move between them to her home. In less than a span, Tama could no longer contain her excitement, bouncing up and down.

"I must go see how my daughter and our new grandchild are doing," she said to any who could hear her.

"Go," Egyptus said. "A grandchild is important. We will finish this."

The backbreaking work of throwing the grains into the breeze, allowing the dirt and loose bits of the plants to blow away while the grains fell back to the earth, took most of the day. It was not until they gathered the last of the cleaned grain into baskets to take to the storage building that Tama returned to the work area.

"I have a grandson," she said. A huge grin lit her face.

"Aker will be a good big brother," Pharoah said. Chayim and Cira are good parents.

"They are," Tama said. "I am blessed to have an honorable daughter and the son of my heart."

"You are blessed," Egyptus said. "I will go visit after we finish with this grain. Does the child have a name yet?"

Tama shook her head. "Mama Gilit wants the child to be named after her papa Shem. Shiblom would like him to be named Afra, after his papa. They have caught poor Cira and Chayim in the middle of the argument."

"I suspect they will choose a different name altogether," Egyptus said as she poured the last of the rye into a basket. "I feel sorry for them. They should not have parents trying to influence the name they choose. Perhaps they would like to use Shiblom or Animim as the name for their son."

Tama grabbed a handle of a basket. "I will help carry this to the storage building. I did not help with the threshing."

Egyptus grabbed the other handle and the two women lifted the basket between them.

"Good thing this is a papyrus basket," Tama said. "I do not think our old baskets would have held this much weight."

"They would have, but they would have been heavier," Egyptus said.

After depositing the rye, they returned to help carry other baskets of grain to the storage building.

"Is the baby beautiful?" Egyptus asked as they carried the basket.

"After we washed him and gave his head time to relax from birth, he is growing more beautiful," Tama said. "Their heads squish during birth."

"They do. Sometimes we must wait for them to relax to see the actual shape."

"It is good this is not Cira's first child. She knows the babe's head changes shape after birth."

"That misshapen?" Egyptus asked.

"He waited too long to be born after dropping low in his mama's body. I remember her concern after Aker's birth. He did the same thing."

"New mamas do not always understand."

"She should have. She saw Gris and Ester as tiny babies," Tama said, helping to lift a basket of wheat. "Perhaps she had not grown enough to remember."

"Young girls often do not," Egyptus said as they set the basket on the floor and turned to go get more.

They worked together with the others until they had stored all the grain inside the storehouse.

"I will wash before I go visit the new baby," Egyptus said.

Tama smiled. "Cira will be happy to see you, Grandmama Egyptus."

"And I will be happy to see her and her little family."

Familiar Stranger

Egyptus enjoyed a few quiet weeks working on more copies of the Book of Commandments for other young couples until the warning sound from the shell echoed through the village once more. Families rove through the valley, many working on the land they had chosen when they first arrived in Egypt.

Egyptus grabbed her staff and hurried to her assigned meeting place. Many of the members of her team were outside the walls and did not come. She heard shouts from outside the wall, from people begging to be allowed in.

The men at the gate must have opened it enough for those outside to enter, for soon more women in Egyptus's group joined her with their staffs while men with their swords and bows rushed up the stairs.

"What is going on outside the wall?" Egyptus asked.

Devora and Jason hurried to their places. Devora stood near Egyptus. "We were returning from our land in the valley when we heard the guard blow on the shell. A group of strange men appeared behind us, running toward the village from the wilderness. We had to race ahead of them to arrive first. Now they are outside the wall, wanting to come in."

Unintelligible sounds came from the men outside the wall. Even though the sounds were unrecognizable, Egyptus understood their intent. They were angry and wanted in.

She desperately wanted to climb the steps to the top of the wall to see who was out there. Perhaps these men did not want to take everything in their little village.

She snorted, doubting that intent.

Cira joined them with her staff. "What was that about?"

"What are you doing here? You have a new baby to protect," Egyptus demanded.

"I am here to protect him. He is with his brother and the other children in the sanctuary. I could not stay in the sanctuary with my children when so many left for their lands today. We will be short people to fight off these men," Cira said, pounding her staff into the ground. "What was that snort for?"

Egyptus shook her head. There was no time to argue. "I thought these men may not want to take everything we have worked so hard to build."

"No chance of that," Marji said.

"Hence my snort," Egyptus said. "I may not understand their words, but I know why they are here. Much as I would like them to want to exchange goods with us, I doubt it is for anything good."

"No chance of that," Marji repeated.

"I know, but I can hope." Egyptus twirled her staff and pounded it into the earth beside her.

"One day they will come to trade," Shim said as he climbed the stairs, "but I doubt it will be today."

"I hope that will happen sooner than later." Egyptus leaned on her staff.

"Perhaps, but it will not be today," Jason said. "Those men are preparing to attack."

"Someday they will not attack," Egyptus whispered, gripping her staff and preparing for the men to scale the wall.

Ester pounded her staff into the earth. "They will not take us today."

She did not have to wait long, for soon a hemp rope bounced against the top of the wall.

"They come," Baraq shouted.

Egyptus glanced around. Only three couples had managed to return to the safety of the village walls. Timor and Alma and Levi and Lexa had not. She whispered a prayer for their safety. Timor and Alma had taken their children with them. She prayed for Jehovah to hide them from discovery and keep all who were still outside the walls safe.

Another two ropes, knotted on the end, bounced against the top of the wall. One slid between two of the new logs and slid down, catching and holding taut. Egyptus sucked in a breath and stabilized her stance. Men would soon appear above the wall.

The three men dropped stones on the attacker's heads and pushed many of them back before they could climb over. Sometimes they beat the enemy's hands with the hilt of their swords, causing them to fall. However, they could not prevent them all from climbing over the wall. The baskets of stones emptied too soon.

Men struggled over the wall to fight the strangers. With only three men to fight them off, the invaders nearly overwhelmed the three men of Egypt.

Egyptus raced up the stairs, her staff held ready to swing into the nearest man. A familiar-looking man met her as he raced toward the stairs. She swung her staff at the man, hitting him on the side of the head. He fell to the walkway without moving.

Swinging her staff and banging hands and heads as they tried to climb over the wall, Egyptus helped the men fight back the attackers. No man who came near her successfully avoided her staff. Maintaining her focus as she fought, Egyptus tried to remember the name of that first man. She should remember the face.

The three couples and Egyptus spent the next span fighting off men who swarmed up the ropes. After many more enemies had climbed the ropes to fight against the men from Egypt and Egyptus, they stopped coming. Of those who made it over the wall, most of their enemies lay on the walkway, unconscious. Two had fallen to the ground where the women had beaten them into submission. No other foes attempted to climb the ropes hanging across the wall.

Egyptus leaned over the wall to look. No men stood or lay at the bottom of the wall. No more noise of attack sounded anywhere outside the walls. Once more, they had overcome their enemies with Jehovah's help.

But who was the familiar man?

Animim hurriedly approached the back wall, hoping to ensure all who fought there were safe, and that none of the invaders had taken any of the women or escaped into the village. "How many men did you fight here? It looks like you fought as many men as we fought at all the other walls together."

Baraq stared at the men lying on the walkway and those on the ground below. "We had a difficult time fighting this many. Levi, Timor, and Chayim did not return to help."

"They fought from outside, attacking our enemies from behind. It split their strength, helping us to fight them off easier at the front gate."

"Too bad none thought to go to the back to fight against these men," Shim said. "Our group was small. We had a difficult time fighting off all the men who climbed the ropes. We would not have prevailed if Egyptus had not run up the stairs to fight with us."

Animim gazed at Egyptus. "You fought here with the men?"

She drew herself up straight and stared at him. "I did. They were becoming overwhelmed and needed my help. If I had not, we would have dead men and women instead of the live ones you see here. Seven is not enough to fight this many men, even if they come at us a few at a time over the wall."

Animim sucked in a deep breath and let it out slowly. "We knew your team had fewer people because the others did not return in time, but we did not realize how small a group you have. I should have sent a runner —"

"What good would a runner have been?" Marji asked, her exhaustion showing in her surly voice. "The boys are not big enough to help us battle these big men."

"No," Animim said, shaking his head. "But the runner could have told us how few of you were here fighting against so many men."

Jason stepped forward. "It does not matter. We fought them off, thanks to the extra help we received from Egyptus. Our attackers are gone, dead, or unconscious."

"Not all," Ester said. "This man is waking. We need to bind him and all the others who still live before they force us to fight them once more."

"We do not want to fight another battle," Baraq agreed.

Marji retrieved lengths of rope from a basket they had stashed beneath the walkway stairs after the last battle. She tossed one to Devora. "You tie that one while I tie this one."

Egyptus and each of the others grabbed a length of rope and bound the men's arms behind their backs, then tied their legs.

"You will not fight us again like that," Egyptus murmured as she pulled the last knot tight.

"Was Ludim captured again?"

Animim shook his head. "He did not come inside, but we heard him shouting at the others from outside."

The man she had hit first groaned. The tall, disheveled, dark-haired man had bruises beginning to show on his face and body. "Why you hit me hard? I came to warn you."

"You attacked us. Who are you?" Egyptus stared at the man. "Why do you look so familiar? And why do I understand the words you speak?"

Jason pulled the man to his feet. "Who are you?" He did not let go of the man's arms.

The man flicked his eyes toward Egyptus. "Ask her. She knows."

"No," Egyptus said. "I do not know you." She stared into his face. "No wait. You are familiar. But only the people who came with me here to Egypt speak our language. Everyone who stayed in Shinar had their language changed, except Mama, Papa, Grandpapa Noah, and a few other obedient people."

"How you know that? You far from Shinar?" the man asked.

"Who are you? I have asked for the last time!" Jason said with a snarl.

The man stared at his feet, his lips thinning as he clenched them together. "I am obedient you speak."

"And who am I, if you know me?" Egyptus demanded.

"You are ..." His eyes flicked to the left, blinking faster than normal. "You are..." He blinked many times before closing them and wrinkling his forehead.

"If you know me, why do you not know my name?" Egyptus asked, working to draw the anger from her voice. She sensed she knew this man, but did not remember him.

"I know you," the man said. "I not remember your name."

"Here is an easier question for you," Animim said. "What is your name? You should know your own name."

The man shook his head slowly back and forth. He squeezed his lips together. "Forgot. That bump ..."

"How do you speak our language?" Cira demanded.

"I, uh, —"

"Tell us. You know how you learned our language," Animim said, his voice low and dangerous.

The man shrank away from him as far as he could, with Jason holding him.

"You know," Animim said.

"I learned ..." The man gazed at the ground, squeezing his lips together. "I not know how."

"You do not know much," Jason said with a growl and shook the man.

"We will see what Pharoah can learn from you," Animim said. "Bring him."

"What about all these other men?" Cira asked. "Those who still live will wake soon."

"I will send others to get them. It will not be long." Animim turned and strode toward the gate. Jason followed, pushing the familiar man forward in small, halting steps caused by his tied legs.

"He looks funny walking like that," Marji said with her first grin since they had gathered to defend against the attack.

"He should look funny," Egyptus said. "I just wish I knew why he looks so familiar." She searched through her memory, seeking and discarding the faces of people she once knew in Shinar.

Men rushed toward the small group of defenders soon after Animim and Jason took the stranger to see Pharoah. As the enemy men awakened from the blows to their heads, they surrounded them, menacing them with their swords.

"You were busy back here," Shiblom said. "We did not have as many attack us at the front gate."

"But we were attacking from behind," Chayim said, hugging Cira. "We drew half of their number back to fight us."

"It is good to see you, Chayim," Egyptus said. "Did you lose any to these attackers?"

"They killed no one, but Jov received an injury. An attacker slashed his arm as he fought against him. Eber joined his battle and they worked together to kill the attacker."

"How many enemies were killed?" Bilhah asked.

"Too many, if we killed even one," Egyptus murmured.

"They attacked us!" Chayim cried. "We did not invade their home. It was not our choice to kill them. They attempted to hurt us and steal from us. I did not like that we had to kill them, but they were in the wrong."

"We killed three who attacked us," Pym said. "If we had not, one or more of us would be dead now."

Egyptus sighed again. "I know, but I hate to have us take the lives of our brothers."

"They are no longer our brothers," Shiblom said, anger filling his voice. "When they attack, they become our enemies."

Egyptus rolled her lips inward and thought about it briefly. "Yes. They became our enemies when they attacked us. I wish they would have tried to learn our language or teach us theirs. Trade would be better for them and us."

Esrom hurried to join the small group surrounding their captured enemies. "Papa wants us to take all the captives to the gathering place by the gate. We can guard them easier there when they are together. And, Grandmama, Papa needs you. He wants you to join him now."

"What would Pharoah want of me?" she murmured. A sudden coldness filled her center.

Did they find Ludim again? Did he direct this attack from outside? What is happening?

"You will find out when you get there," Esrom said.

"Probably he has something to tell you about the strange man who speaks our language," Bilhah said.

Egyptus nodded. "You are probably correct." She left the group and trotted across the village to the gathering place near the front gate, carrying her staff in the ready position, ready for another fight.

You never know when someone will break away.

As she neared the gate, she heard men shouting. The stranger must have said something they did not like.

Who is he?

She came around Animim's home and slowed her pace, listening to the jeers and shouting from the men. She searched her memory, trying to remember how she knew this strange man.

Shaking her head, she joined Pharoah. "You wanted to see me?"

"Mama! Yes. Animim told me this man seems to know you. How?"

"I hit him across the head when he attacked us. Perhaps he remembers that."

"No. There is something more."

"Has he said anything useful?" Egyptus stared at the stranger surrounded by a circle of many village men. "Should those men be guarding our other prisoners?"

Pharoah gave her a curt nod and called out. "You men need to be guarding all our prisoners, not heckling this one."

The men stepped away and turned toward the other prisoners. Animim and Jason stayed near the stranger.

"What did he say to draw such anger from the men?" Egyptus asked.

"He said he is one who honors Jehovah."

"That could be," Egyptus mumbled. "But why did he attack us from the back of the village with the others? Why did he say he was here to warn us?"

"That is my question," Pharoah said. "He is hiding something. I do not know what, but I do not trust him."

"Nor do I," Egyptus said. "He is familiar to me, but why? How do I know him?"

"More importantly," Pharoah added, "how does he understand and speak our language?"

"That is what bothers me. He looks familiar, too familiar. He is not my brother. I doubt he is a child of Shem, how did he learn our language?"

"And if he is one of them, why is he with our enemies?"

Egyptus sighed. "He is a puzzle."

"A puzzle we need to solve, and quickly. Come with me. Perhaps you can spark a memory in him." Pharoah walked toward the stranger.

Egyptus skipped two steps to catch up and take Pharoah's elbow. "Or he will tell us more lies. I kept expecting him to open his mouth and speak the truth, but he clamped the words in."

"I saw that as well. He acted like it was all he could do to hold the truth in and not share it."

"I have a hard time trusting him."

"Shush now, Mama. We are too close to him. We do not want him to hear us."

**

Egyptus trod the final distance in silence, staring intently at the strange man. He continued to look familiar, but why?

"There you are!" the man cried. "I look you."

Egyptus refused to answer him, waiting for Pharoah to signal she should speak.

"Why do you search for this woman?" Pharoah asked

The stranger stared from Egyptus to Pharoah. "She special. She knows curse."

"The curse? What curse do you speak of?" Animim asked.

"Jehovah curse people Shinar, not stop tower."

They were cursed! My dreams were visions.

"You were cursed?" Pharoah asked. "There was no curse when we left there."

"I do not believe there was a curse," Animim said. "What curse did Jehovah send? Did he send rain to wash away the tower?"

"Jehovah could not," the man said with a taunting laugh. "Noah say flooded earth, but myth, like Adam and Eve."

The flood is no myth. My mama and papa survived it with Grandpapa Noah and Grandmama Imma! This man must be generations younger than me.

"The flood is a myth? You do not believe Noah and his sons?" Animim asked, jerking on the cords that bound the stranger's arms.

"Do not!" the man cried. "Hurts."

"Do not lie," Animim said.

"How did Jehovah curse you? Or were you not cursed?" Pharoah asked.

"I cursed, all Shinar cursed. That scourge to mankind thought control us."

Scourge? He calls our God a scourge? Jerk on those cords again. No, do not. I cannot be uncharitable.

"Scourge? Do you mean Jehovah?" Jason asked.

"Yes. He knew could not build tower if could not talk. Mixed up the language every man. No one understand. Some families, even husband, wife not understand."

We have never seen that.

"How can we believe you?" Pharoah demanded. "You speak the same words we speak."

"That I say Ludim —," he clapped a hand over his mouth.

"Ludim?" Pharoah asked. "Who is this Ludim?"

Ludim! He knows Ludim?

"Woman know," the stranger said, pointing to Egypt. "Why you not speak?"

"Who is this Ludim you speak of?" Animim asked, cocking his head to the side. "I know of no Ludim."

"Lived Shinar. Led one building team on tower. I respected him."

"How can he tell you anything if Jehovah altered and mixed up everyone's words?" Pharoah asked, furrowing his brow.

"I ..." the man rolled his lips close and glanced away, his eyes blinking faster. "I not say understand Ludim."

Pharoah lifted his chin. "Oh?"

"I not lie!" the stranger shouted.

"I did not accuse you of telling an untruth," Pharoah said in his quiet, level voice.

Egyptus could smell barbed fear exude from the man. *He knows Ludim. And he knows we know he knows.*

"But what did this Ludim tell you to say?" Animim asked, pursing his lips.

"He not say anything me. He not. We not speak."

"Why did he send you here with the other attackers?" Pharoah asked.

"He thought ... No. You cannot deceive."

"Perhaps," Pharoah said with a nod. "You are an intelligent man. I cannot trust you until you determine to speak the truth."

"I speak truth!" the man protested.

"What is your name? It would be easier to speak to you if we know your name," Animim asked.

"My name ..." he paused with his lips pressed tightly together once more. "I not remember name. You remember name?" He gazed at Egyptus.

She shook her head and shrugged, determined not to speak to the man.

"You remember your name," Animim encouraged. "I see it on your lips, waiting to slip out."

"I ... I ... I not remember!" the stranger cried.

Pharoah sighed. "Then we will call you Cain. We cannot call you 'that strange man'."

"Cain? Why you call me Cain?" the man asked with a little shake of his head.

"Cain was a wicked man. You seem to be a wicked man. You show nothing different." Pharoah turned and took Egyptus by the elbow. "Come with me. Cain does not wish to speak the truth."

They strode away from the man now called Cain, ignoring his clamoring for attention.

Pharoah turned on his heel. "You are welcome to gag Cain."

Animim whipped out a white cloth from his pocket and tucked it into Cain's mouth, tying it behind his head. Mumbled words were all that came from him after that.

Pharoah and Egyptus walked a distance before stopping to speak.

"What do you think, Mama?" Pharoah asked. "What is wrong with his story?"

"He says he knows Ludim and was told something by him. But he is unwilling to share what he was told. He keeps stopping, as though he is unable to speak the words he thinks."

"Do you think he has been enchanted?"

"It is possible."

"What can we do to break the enchantment?" Pharoah asked.

"I do not know. Other than pray for him. But I do not know if I want to do that. He seems to hate Jehovah." Egyptus tilted her head to the side and pursed her lips. "How can one hate their God?"

"It is difficult to understand," Pharoah agreed.

Expulsion

The men had gathered all their captured enemies, except Cain, into a circle, forcing them to kneel facing out, away from each other.

Egyptus could hear them mumbling in their strange language as she stared at them from a distance. Some words sounded familiar, but not many. None made any sense.

How could this Cain have learned to speak their language?

They had lived in peace three months before this attack. What would Pharoah do with these men? There was no longer a surplus of food in their storehouses.

Although they had recently harvested the fields, there was little more than what the growing community would need to feed themselves and have seed for the next year, with a little extra in case of drought.

The rains had not stopped falling each year, but Egyptus had read about droughts in the books written by the ancient matriarchs. She did not want to eat all the seed they would need for the next year.

They could not do as they had after the last attack. The storehouses did not hold enough food to give to these enemies before driving them away as they had with Ludim. Why did these enemies return?

The potent stench of fear filled the green. *Did it come from the captured enemy or from the people of Egypt?*

Probably both.

"Food?" a man in the circle asked.

"Food?" another man asked.

Most of the men in the circle spoke the word in a chant. "Food, food, food."

"Where did these men learn that word?" Egyptus asked.

"We gave our enemies food last time they attacked," Pharoah said. "I wondered then if it was the right thing to do."

"What will you do this time? These men attacked and tried to kill us."

"I know. We cannot send them off with food. It makes them think we will feed them if they attack us."

Egyptus and Pharoah stared at the prisoners for a time. "So what will you do?" she repeated.

"I will ask the women to guard these men while we discuss the problem."

"Will we women not have any wisdom to offer?" Egyptus asked.

"You will, but we need someone to guard the prisoners." Pharoah kicked the dirt with his toe. "What do you suggest?"

"You can meet with half of the men and women while the others guard the prisoners. Then we can trade. That way, everyone will have a say in the solution."

"But they will miss some of the discussion," Pharoah argued.

"Send all but a a few at a time and trade the guards out during the discussion. Do not bring husbands with wives, so they can share what they heard with the other." Egyptus stared at the prisoners. "But do not let that Cain, who knows our language, come close to your discussions, nor allow him too close to the others. He understands more than he professes."

Pharoah nodded and ran his hands through his hair. "I agree. I will have to get men I trust to guard him without allowing his words to tempt them while we discuss the problem. I do not trust him."

"Nor do I. I suggest you keep him gagged."

Pharoah strode to Meyer and Moren and spoke quietly with them, waving once or twice toward Cain and his guards.

Moren strode to the small circle of men and tapped Jason on the shoulder. He whispered to him before Jason walked away, shaking his arms to relieve the stress. Meyer soon relieved Animim. Arvad joined the little circle around Cain.

Pharoah walked through the group of men and women who stood guard around the enemy prisoners. Soon, women stepped in to take the place of some men who left. The released men moved toward the back of the village green to meet.

Egyptus strolled toward the prisoners to take her turn to guard.

Pharoah caught her by the arm. "No, Mama. I need you to come to the meeting and be sure we restate everything said earlier for those who come late. People trust your wisdom and honesty. And I do not want you close to those men. Something warns me against it."

Egyptus nodded and turned on her heel to join those who strode toward the meeting place. They usually held these meetings in the sanctuary, but this time Pharoah must have wanted to stay close to his prisoners.

"We must decide what to do with these men," Pharoah said when all had gathered with no other words of explanation.

"Why can we not do as we did last time?" Gilit asked.

"Give them food and drive them away?" Kib asked.

"What good would that do us?" Alma asked.

"They would be gone from our village. Those last ones did not return," Gilit said, folding her arms in front of her.

"No?" Levi asked. "I drove them out. Some of those men are here again. I recognize them."

"And I heard Ludim's voice outside the village walls," Shule said.

"It did nothing more than teach them we will feed them if they attack us," Xenia said.

"Then what should we do?" Pharoah asked.

"We cannot kill them. That is what Mama said," Magda offered. "Although I see no reason not to kill them. They wanted to kill us."

"Some tried," Jov said, holding his bandaged arm close to his body. "The one who cut my arm tried to kill me."

"And you killed him for the effort," Timor said.

"I did. I would do it again," Jov said.

"That is what worries me," Egyptus whispered to herself. *And suffer for the crime of killing another man.*

"What did you say, Mama?" Pharoah asked. "I asked you to be here because of your experience."

"I have no more experience with attacking enemies than you," Egyptus said. "But I fear our men will learn to enjoy killing. They have not yet killed us. We cannot be like our enemy. We cannot kill because we can."

"But they returned when we told them to stay away!" Jason cried.

"I know. But we fed them. We gave them a reason to return." Egyptus set a hand on her hip. "You would return if you were hungry."

"I would," Jason agreed.

"If we do not feed them, what do we do?" Isa asked.

All eyes turned to Egyptus.

After everyone had moved between guarding the men and taking part in the discussion, everyone agreed on a resolution to the problem. Gilit had argued against it, but had reluctantly agreed.

Magda found cloths to use for blindfolds and gags, although Ester strongly suggested they use papyrus, claiming the stickiness would make them think twice about returning.

"Next time they return, they get papyrus," Xenia said.

"There had better not be a next time," Pharoah said with a growl.

When Egyptus joined the others surrounding the prisoners on the other end of the village green, a stench of stale sweat and fear seemed almost to color the air around the prisoners. She sniffed and rubbed her nose with a shudder.

The villagers checked to ensure that all the bindings were tight on each man, then lifted them into the back of the wagon Esrom had brought. Egyptus took some of the cloths from Magda, as did Isa and Tama, and tied them around the eyes of each man, holding their breath as much as possible to avoid inhaling their putrid odor.

"Are they taking Cain?" Isa asked in a whisper, nodding toward the man who sat away from the others.

"I would like to learn how he speaks our language before we send him away, but Pharoah thinks that is too dangerous," Egyptus replied as quietly to her friend. "So, yes. They will take Cain with them. I fear, however, it will be as dangerous to send him away as it is to keep him here. He is a dangerous man."

"And evil. I sense his evil when I am near him." Isa shuddered. "I am glad Pharoah decided to send him with the others."

"He is not going with the others. They are taking him separately in a different wagon and in the opposite direction. There is no need for us to help him destroy us."

Isa nodded as she pulled another blindfold tight and knotted it behind the man's head.

Silently they finished blindfolding the men, then stood back to watch each prisoner be lifted into the wagon. They had gagged the noisier men to stop their shouting complaints. There were more enemies this time. They must have shared the idea that if they survived, the people of Egypt would feed them. They were wrong. The people of Egypt would not feed them.

Not this time.

Never again.

Emer, Meyer, and Akish climbed into the wagon with the prisoners while Levi sat in the seat to guide the mules.

Animim, Jason, Arvad, and Baraq silently settled into the back of the second wagon with Cain. Iram had convinced Pharoah he could drive the horses of this wagon.

Jov and Kashet held the gate open as the two wagons creaked through. They banged it closed, bringing the locking bar down before running up the stairs to join Egyptus and the others on the wall to watch them drive away.

Levi guided his mules northwest, taking them back in the direction those in Egypt had followed to reach their new home. Iram, however, directed his horses to cross the Black River and took Cain away to the east.

When both wagons had driven out of sight, people spoke again.

"Why were we warned not to speak while the prisoners were here?" Gilit asked.

"You know," Pharoah said. "You were at all the meeting. We do not want them to know our plans and intentions. They do not need to know who is with them and who is not. Nor do they need to know they are not getting food. They went peaceably, thinking we would feed them at the end of the ride."

"But I do not understand taking the one you call Cain so far the other way," Gilit whined.

"Why do you care?" Chana asked. "Is he someone you know?"

Gilit glanced away and bit down on her lower lip. "No." She paused a long breath before continuing. "I do not like to see him sent off on his own."

What does she know? Who is this Cain that she cares?

"He will find others to join," Jakob said with a growl. "Men like him are seldom alone. They find others to do their bidding."

"Or the one whose bidding he does," Isa breathed into Egyptus's ear.

In a voice barely above the sound of a soft breeze, Egyptus replied. "You think someone enchanted him too?" She gazed into Isa's eyes to see the answer.

"Yes, he was enchanted. His eyes are not right." She then lifted her voice so others could hear. "It is good to have him out of our village, but I fear Cain will return with more enemies."

"And with a knowledge of our defense. I need to speak to Pharoah. We must change our defense plans to surprise the next band of attacking enemies."

Isa nodded and Egyptus strode down the walkway to find Pharoah.

"We must talk," she said when she reached him.

"Is it important? Can we speak here or ...?"

"Yes, it is important," Egyptus said. "Xenia can hear, but for now, I would rather not share with the others."

Pharoah nodded and led Xenia down the stairs toward the sanctuary. Egyptus stopped them under the banyan tree near the center of the green. She peered into the tree and saw no children sitting in its branches before she spoke.

"We can talk here. No one will overhear us," she said.

"Why are you being secretive?" Xenia asked.

"Isa and I shared some thoughts," Egyptus said. "Someone enchanted the man you called Cain."

"Enchanted?" Xenia said with a harsh laugh.

"I thought he was," Pharoah said. "How do you know?"

"Isa saw it in his eyes. He will bring others here to fight us. He has seen how we fight and where we place our strongest warriors."

"What are you suggesting?" Pharoah asked.

"We must move our people around, change our fighting style —"

"Make it different, harder for them to defeat," Pharoah said, nodding. "Yes."

"But why did you have to say this away from the others?" Xenia asked.

"There are some I do not trust," Egyptus said.

"After everything we have suffered together, you do not trust everyone in Egypt?" Xenia asked, staring at the mother of her heart like she had grown two heads.

"No. Someone here is sharing information," Egyptus said.

Changes

While waiting for the wagons to return from depositing their enemies far away, men dug a vast hole outside the walls of the village. Into this, they dumped the bodies of the dead. The residents of Egypt joined Pharoah in praying for the souls of those who had attempted to kill them.

A few people stood on the walkways, watching out for more attackers as the others participated in the burial. As they completed their prayers over their dead enemies, a woman shouted from the walkway, pointing west.

Egyptus joined others who scurried up the stairs of the walkway for a better view. A thin trail of dust rose in the distance.

Soon the donkeys pulling the wagon that took most of the enemy men away became visible. It did not take long to see the men riding in the wagon. Levi sagged at the reins.

Before this wagon reached the gate, a man shouted and pointed east. Egyptus turned in time to see the horses and wagon that had carried Cain and his guards. The horses plodded along almost as slowly as the mules.

The men in that wagon grew larger as the wagon inched closer. Iram slumped in his wagon seat, looking exhausted from the travel across an area where men rarely traveled. It had been a long day: fighting the enemy, resolving the problems of the captured men, and taking them away.

Egyptus expected the need to drive wagons across long distances to the west to change soon. Eber and his friends would have boats floating up and down the river and in the other streams that lead to the salt sea they called the Siddim. Perhaps they would even travel upriver to the south and discover new lands and peoples there.

A shudder ran up Egyptus's spine.

Would the new people we meet treat us as enemies and our visit as an attack? Would they try to kill us? Our people would not attack those city walls and try to enter without permission. Why did men coming to Egypt think they had to force their way in without even trying to knock on the gate? I will have to remember to remind any who travel to other parts of the land to be more polite than these enemy attackers have been.

The wagons reached the gate one after the other and rolled through and back to the barns where the animals lived. There, the men leapt from the wagons and helped unhitch the animals, brushing and feeding them. Others joined them to push the wagons beneath the shelter to protect them from rain.

Egyptus entered the barn in time to see Iram slump next to the horse he groomed. She ran to his side.

"Are you well?"

"The trip there and back was rougher than I expected," Iram mumbled. "There were no wagon tracks to follow, only a few trails made by the animals."

"Did Cain argue any?" Pharoah asked as he and Xenia joined the men in the barn.

"He tried to speak through his gag, but Animim pushed it back in and added another over the top," Jason said from beside another horse. "He could not say much after that. By the time we finally stopped, he seemed to sleep."

"Did he speak or say anything when you left him there on his own?" Pharoah asked.

"He made little noise as we lifted him out of the wagon and set him on a rock. I built a low fire to protect him from wild beasts," Arvad said with a frown. "I doubt he appreciates the gift. He did not see the big cats crouching in the distance. He will deserve it if they catch him."

"Arvad!" Egyptus cried.

"I am sorry, Mama Egyptus," Arvad said, though his voice did not sound contrite. "I should not wish bad things on the animals. His evil would sicken them."

"Did they attack him?" Xenia asked, sucking in a deep breath.

"I do not know. He did not scream while we were close enough to hear. I do not know if I even care. That man oozes evil."

Egyptus's eyebrows shot up. "Evil?"

Iram lifted his head from the side of the horse he brushed. "He is slimy like the black mud from the Black River. It scared me to have him behind me, even with Arvad and the others beside him. I breathed easier when we left him behind. The big cats do not make me as nervous as that man."

"Your papa should not have allowed you to go," Xenia said.

"No, Mama." Iram brushed the horse and clouds of dust rose from its side. "I asked to go. I am old enough to do this. It frightened me, but I needed to go. I can do hard things. I need to pray and thank Jehovah for getting us there and home safely."

"We all need to pray and thank Jehovah for our safety," Pharoah said. "Do you have the strength to walk to the sanctuary? Someone else can groom this horse."

Iram stiffened his back. "No, Papa. I can finish grooming this horse. I will join you in the sanctuary soon."

Animim lifted his eyebrows as he looked at the boy. "I have a horse to groom before I can leave. I will be here with Iram. We will join you in the sanctuary soon. Go gather the rest of the village."

Pharoah gazed around at the others who groomed tired animals. "Join us in the sanctuary as soon as you can.".

He took Xenia and Egypt by the elbows and walked outside with them.

"I will gather the others. Meet us there," he said.

"Do you need —" Egyptus started.

"No, Mama. I can do it. I will get others to help. You and Xenia go wait for us."

Xenia turned to get her younger children from the house before joining Egyptus and the others who slowly gathered in the sanctuary. People spoke in quiet voices, remembering they had gathered in a holy space.

The returning men slowly drifted in to join them, followed at last by Animim walking with an arm around Iram, holding him up.

They moved to the front where Egyptus waited with Xenia and her family.

"You did a good job, son. You will be a good man," Animim murmured.

Iram nodded.

Lim put an arm around him and helped the boy kneel. Xenia knelt beside him on the other side to hold him upright.

Pharoah called the community to kneel and lifted his hands. "Most Gracious Jehovah," he intoned. "We are grateful ..."

The women spent the next morning practice working harder than ever with their staffs. Not all women joined, but most did. Gilit, as usual, did not. Some noted the absences of those who did not come to practice.

Egyptus dropped to the ground from exertion with the others at the end of the first dance with the staff.

"Why do Gilit and Isa not join us?" Hulda asked, plopping to the ground near her mama.

"Isa is still attending to our injured from yesterday's attack," Magda said, still breathing hard. "Jov's arm has become infected. The man who attacked him must have used some poison on his sword."

"Poison?" Bilhah cried. "Why would they do that? Is it not enough they attack us?"

"They are becoming more serious about trying to hurt us," Ada said, still panting from the faster pace of the dance. "They no longer want to only steal our food and our women. Now they want to hurt us and kill our men."

"Isa has a reason to be gone, but where is Gilit? Where is Elsa?" Hulda asked.

"Elsa is Gilit's daughter. She would listen to her mama's hatred," Bilhah said.

"No," Xenia said. "Elsa is in bed after yesterday's trying day. She is trying to stop the loss of their next child. All the excitement and action of fighting against the intruders caused her to have some trouble."

"Elsa is with child again?" Cira asked.

"I did not know she carries another," Lexa said.

"She has kept the knowledge of the child to herself and her family. She struggles to keep them within her until time for their birth," Xenia said, rising from the ground, using her staff to push her up. "She does not want the extra attention."

"She will get it whether or not she wants it," Lexa said as she stood. "We want her to keep her babies." She moved to her position, prepared to practice the dance again.

"It will embarrass —" Xenia said.

"She will love our attention," Cira said.

Hulda led them in the dance once more. While Egyptus went through the movements that had become natural to her many years before, she thought about Gilit, who had never thought it necessary to join in the practices. Did she even have a staff? She would be in trouble if an enemy got past the others and found her alone.

She shrugged. They forced no one to join in the early morning practice. Whatever happened to Gilit would be her problem.

She stumbled over her staff and groaned. *Time to pay attention.* Glancing around to be certain none of the others noticed, she stopped thinking about Gilit and focused on the movements of the dance.

Hulda had sped up once more. Egyptus's staff moved smoothly around her as she went through the steps.

As she sat to rest the next time, Magda winked at her. Egyptus lifted a shoulder, then glanced around the group of women. "We need to improve our practice, get better at what we do."

"Why?" Bilhah asked.

"Some men who attacked us yesterday were men who were here before. They know how we defend against them. They will be better prepared to attack us next time."

"Is there something else we can use to fight against them besides these staffs?" Dora asked, pounding her staff into the ground. "I love using my staff. It has helped keep men away from me during our recent attacks. But, is there something different, something our enemy would not expect?"

"I read my grandmamas used swords and sharp hair pins they threw at their enemies," Egyptus said. "Before you ask, I do not know what they looked like or how they worked."

"We can use swords if we have them," Magda said.

"But who among us has a sword?" Lexa asked.

"I do," Egyptus said.

"So do I," Magda and several others chimed in, raising their hands.

"How do we get a sword if we do not have one?" Devora asked.

"Some of your husbands may have more than one sword," Bilhah said.

"There are those left from the men who attacked us yesterday," Alma said.

"But the boys claimed them," Cira said, pounding her knee with her fist. "We need them more than the young boys. It is us the attackers will take, not the boys."

"They will take the boys as slaves. They need to learn to protect themselves too," Xenia said.

"We should ask Pharoah about that," Chana said.

The women turned toward Egyptus.

"Why look at me?" she asked.

"Pharoah is your son," Hulda said.

"And your brother. And Xenia's husband. I am not the only one who can talk to Pharoah."

"But you are the true leader of Egypt," Ada said. "He listens to your counsel."

Other women added their comments to those of Ada, all encouraging Egyptus to be the one to talk with Pharoah.

Egyptus threw her hands into the air, causing her staff to bounce in her hands. "I will do it. But what we need most is a way to make more swords."

"Do any of our men know how to do that?" Chana asked.

"I do not know. I have not asked," Egyptus said. "No one has made new swords since we arrived, at least none that I know. Do any of you have husbands who can make swords?"

No one spoke up or raised their hand. "We need to find someone who can make swords," Magda said.

"Or someone willing to try if he does not," Devora said.

"We need him, and we need him soon," Egyptus agreed. "I hope we have someone here who has hidden his talent."

Swords and Knives

Magda and Hulda went with Egyptus to see Pharoah after they completed their staff practice.

"I was wondering who would come with you to talk with me, Mama," Pharoah said after asking them to sit in his office. "I knew they would draft you to come talk to me. What ideas do you have to fight against our next attack?"

"We women, need a better way to fight our attackers," Magda said.

"What do you need?" Pharoah asked. He crossed his legs and leaned back in his chair.

Magda folded her arms across her chest. "Our staffs are good, but they do not protect us from our enemy's swords. We need swords."

Pharoah nodded. "We have few swords here in Egypt."

"We do not have enough swords for all the women to learn how to use them. That is the problem," Egyptus said.

"That is the problem for all of us. Even with the swords we took from our enemies, we do not have enough swords for all the men. The boys think they need swords as well." Pharoah set both feet on the floor and leaned forward.

"Men need swords. Their needs are greater than ours," Hulda said.

"Usually," Egyptus murmured.

"What do you mean?" Hulda asked, turning her gaze to her mama. "In our fighting groups, women fight from the ground, men fight the enemy as they climb over the wall."

Egyptus swallowed as the eyes of her children turned on her. "They do in our group as well, when there are enough men to fight. Because of our limited numbers, I ran up the steps to help the men fight on the walkway yesterday."

"You did what?" All three of her children chorused.

She cleared her throat. "There were only three men inside our walls. The others did not make it back in time. The enemy overran our position at the back of the village. Perhaps someone told the enemy of our small fighting group in the back." Egyptus lifted a shoulder in a small shrug. "Someone had to help them."

"So you climbed the stairs to do that?" Magda asked.

Egyptus shrugged. "If not me, who?"

"A man from another assignment," Hulda said, her voice rising.

"Who? Our assignment is the back wall. Every other man inside the walls was busy fighting off the enemy in their assigned position or caught outside and fighting from the rear. We have no women in my group with enough practice to be on the front line. And, because they are mothers with young babies, or carrying new little ones, I would not allow them to go on the walkway. I have no one depending on me."

"No one?" Hulda asked, her voice lifting in pitch.

"What about me," Magda asked, "and Pharoah, and Hulda and all the rest of your children and grandchildren?"

"And all the others who live here in Egypt because they came with you?" Pharoah asked. "We all depend on you."

"I received no injury," Egyptus said, running her hands through her hair.

"That will change," Pharoah said. "Who is in your fighting group?"

"Lexa, Cira, who just had a baby, Ester, Devora, Marji and Alma," Egyptus said, ticking their names off on her fingers. "Only Alma has any experience, but she only began to practice after we settled in Egypt."

Pharoah scratched his head behind his ear. "Your group needs more experienced men. You must have —"

"Levi, Chayim, Jason, Baraq, Shim, Timor, and Esrom," Egyptus listed.

"All but Timor are young men who have not had enough testing," Pharoah said.

"We work well together. Yesterday was more difficult because Chayim, Levi, and Timor did not return in time to fight with us. I do not know what happened to Esrom," Egyptus said, tapping her foot against the floor. "Was it much the same for the other fighting groups?"

"It was," Magda said. "Our group was smaller than usual because so many had gone to work on their land."

"I pulled Esrom to help me run messages since so many were gone. I did not know you had so few men. We were blessed yesterday," Pharoah said. "Our people came to our aid and fought the enemy from behind. Sadly, none went to the back wall."

"The enemy at the front gate probably kept them busy," Egyptus said.

"Most likely," Pharoah murmured. "We need to plan for that. It will happen again."

"That is for you to discuss with the group leaders," Hulda said. "What about swords for the women?"

"Will there be someone to teach you?" Pharoah asked.

Egyptus sucked in a quiet breath and let it out. "You know I can teach the women how to use the sword. I helped your papa teach you. I have used one for many years. I have a sword and have worked with it since I was young," Egyptus said, crossing her feet at the ankles.

"I watched you practice when I was little," Pharoah said.

"I remember that too," both Magda and Hulda said.

"It amazed us you could swing that heavy sword around the way you do and not get cut," Hulda added.

"I tried to pick it up once, but I could not," Magda said. "It was too heavy. How do you do it?"

"It comes from practice," Egyptus said. She leaned forward.

"Swords are heavy," Pharoah said.

"But will there be swords for all the women to use?" Magda asked.

"We need to count the number of swords that have made their way into Egypt. All the older men brought swords with them," Pharoah said, setting his hands on his knees.

"So did many women," Egyptus said.

"We have collected swords from the enemies who attacked us," Pharoah said. "I have given these to the young men who did not have one when we left Shinar. The older boys clamor for the swords left behind by these last attackers, but I have not assigned them."

"Is there someone here in Egypt who knows how to make swords?" Hulda asked. Egyptus could read the yearning for a sword on her face, as she had felt before Afra gave her a sword to use. "If someone could make new swords, we would be in less trouble."

"Make swords?" Pharoah mused, leaning back in his seat. "I have never considered that. I wonder ..."

"We talked about it this morning at our practice," Magda said. "No one shared any knowledge of her husband knowing how to make swords."

"Perhaps no one does. I hope there is one who does," Pharoah said. "I will ask the men when we meet today."

"You will never believe who learned to make swords as a young man," Xenia bubbled the next morning at staff practice.

"Who?" the other women begged.

Egyptus stood on the edge of the circle, watching Xenia enjoy the attention the wife of the leader of a village deserved, and waiting to hear who knew how to make swords.

"Moren," Xenia said.

"Moren!" Several women gasped. "His wife is a healer and he makes swords? No wonder no one knows of his skill."

"I wonder what other skills our men are hiding," Alma said.

"I do not know that," Xenia said, taking back the women's attention. Egyptus allowed her to have it. Too often they deferred to her rather than to Xenia, the wife of Pharoah and leader of Egypt. "Pharoah says he has not made a sword in many years. However, if he can find the right metals, he thinks his hands can remember the skill."

Egyptus thought back to the days when she and Afra were a young couple. Afra would go to Moren's home and watch Moren work on making swords.

Why did I not remember this before? Perhaps because I did not want to remember those times with Afra. Sometimes it hurts to remember. I should have remembered.

"Did you not know, Mama?" Rebecca asked. "Isa is your friend and has been for many years before we left Shinar. Would you not have known her husband makes swords?"

"It has been many years since he made swords. I forgot he did. He became a farmer and a beekeeper to help Isa with her remedies. He wanted to avoid making instruments of death."

"Would he not also make knives? We all need belt knives," Ganet asked, fingering the knife tucked into her belt.

"He did, but he quit. I did not ask why. It was a man's choice and there were many others who made knives in Shinar." Egyptus lifted her shoulders in a small shrug.

"Will he make swords for us women?" Cira asked.

Xenia shook her head and lifted her hands. "Not yet. He must find the metal he needs to make swords and knives. He is a man. He cannot make something from nothing."

The women tittered at the little joke.

"Who here has a sword?" Egyptus asked. "It will help Moren if he does not have to make more swords than necessary."

Hands lifted in the air, mostly women who had married before they trekked from Shinar to Egypt. Egyptus counted the hands.

"Less than half of you have them. If you bring your sword with you tomorrow, I will see how your training has progressed."

"Until we have swords to practice with," Magda said, "we should begin our staff practice."

The women formed lines and moved to the dance of the staff slowly to warm up their muscles. As their muscles warmed, the dance increased in tempo until they were moving in a near blur.

One by one, women dropped out, falling to the ground as the speed increased faster than they had ever practiced before. Finally, only Ava, Chana, and Egyptus continued, although even Magda had fallen to the ground. At last, they stopped and dropped to the ground, panting.

"Why did you speed the dance up so fast?" Lexa asked.

"To see what you would do if more than one man attacks you," Magda said. "We cannot expect the men to wait for us to remember what is next. It must come naturally."

"Why did you not warn us?" Cira asked.

"It would not help you prepare for an enemy if I had warned you," Magda said. "Now, on your feet. The enemy will not wait. Time to spar."

The women found partners and sparred.

"Ouch!" Marji cried when Devora's staff hit her. "You do not need to hit me so hard."

"We were told to fight as if you are the enemy," Devora said. "I would not pull back the strength of my blows if you were the enemy."

"Hold!" Magda called. She waited for all the women to stop sparring. "Gather around."

The women formed a semi-circle around her.

"We need to practice like we are fighting the enemy, but we cannot hurt our sisters. What can we do to protect ourselves?" Magda asked.

The women around her murmured their agreement while rubbing arms and legs that would soon show bruises.

"We need pads to protect our bodies," Rebecca called.

"We can use pads here, but we will not have them when the enemy attacks," Alma said. "We need to be strong, to accept a few bruises."

"But there is no need to bruise and hurt each other now," Magda said.

Egyptus sat on the outside edge of the circle listening to the discussion. When she had started learning to use the sword, they did not use pads to protect their bodies. Instead, they had used wooden swords and received bruises. The wooden swords weighed almost the same as the metal swords and had a similar feel to the actual swords they used later. They were safer for practicing and learning.

She struggled to wait for their decision of how to make protective clothing before she joined the discussion. She would not wear any padding. They could, but she had lived this long with the aches and pains of someone hitting too hard. She did not need to cover her body with pads.

When the women had decided on a padding to wear during the practice and who would make it, Egyptus rose and stepped through the circle of women to the center.

"We need to learn how to use swords, but swords are sharp and more dangerous than our staffs. Even your padding will not protect you from the sharp edges. We can all begin our lessons in using swords the way I did years ago."

"What did you use?" Bilhah asked.

"We learned with wooden swords. I suspect there are men who can help us make practice swords. By the time Moren finds the metals he needs to make swords, we will be prepared to practice fighting with them. We will be ahead of the older boys who think they have all the rights to the swords left behind by our enemies."

The women buzzed with excitement at the thought of wooden practice swords.

"Who will make them?" Hibah asked.

"I will discuss that with Pharoah. He should have practice swords already created for men," Egyptus said.

"I will go with you," Xenia said.

As the two women picked up their staffs, Ester spoke up. "Before you leave, I have a suggestion."

Egyptus and Xenia turned to face the young woman.

"When Ganet mentioned our belt knives, I wondered why we do not learn how to fight with them. We always carry a knife with us."

"To use a knife, you must be very close," Alma said.

"If we get that close, we would need to know how to use the knife to protect ourselves," Ester said. "I have seen the boys throwing their belt knives. Could we not practice throwing them at targets? Then we would not need to be so close to the enemy."

"After you throw your knife, it is gone," Hulda said. "Then what do you do when an enemy comes close?"

"Maybe have a knife hidden in our shoe? Or another in our belt?" Lexa suggested. "I like this idea. We all have knives. We should learn now how to throw them and how to fight with them."

"It will be difficult to do in battle," Ada warned.

"We should know how, though," Egyptus said, surprising the others. "I like your idea, Ester. We should learn how to protect ourselves with the one weapon we always have with us."

The women around her murmured their agreement.

"I do not like thinking about cutting a man who is close to me," Hulda said.

"But it is better than having him take you and do things you would not like," Chana said.

"Yes," Hulda said, dragging out the word. "I do not like to think about it, but we must learn that skill as well. Perhaps you can request someone to teach us about this when you speak to Pharoah?"

Xenia nodded and thrust her staff into the soil. Egyptus lifted hers, ready for trouble as always when she carried her staff. She never used it for a walking stick. She needed to always remember it was a tool, a weapon.

Together, the two women turned toward the other end of the village green where the men and boys practiced.

Learning

E gyptus and Xenia found Pharoah sparring with Timor in a field behind the barn where the men practiced. The spicy odor of men who had been working hard filled the air. They fought with their sharp swords, as men did. The women stood back, watching.

"Watch how they follow through with their swings and slashes," Egyptus said. "They do not allow their sword or arm to halt because it hit an enemy. We do this with our staffs. That is why we practice the dance, to help us keep our staffs swinging. The men allow their swords to keep moving so it will go through their enemy."

"Ooh. I do not like the thought of that," Xenia said, setting a hand on her stomach.

"No, but you would rather have it go through your enemy than have his sword go through you," Egyptus said.

"We should have two men practice for us and give us tips as they practice, and you tell us what is happening."

"That makes sense. It is easier to learn if you can watch another who is skilled. We can ask Pharoah about that."

Upon noticing the women watching them, Pharoah and Timor stopped sparring. They sheathed their swords and joined them.

"Did you women need something?" Timor asked as he walked toward them.

"We do," Xenia said. "Why are you using your sharp swords rather than wooden practice swords?"

"We used wooden practice swords when we were learning," Timor said. "Now that we are proficient with the sword, we must use the real ones to maintain our skills."

"Do you still have wooden ones?" Egyptus asked. "Certainly you need some to teach the older boys and young men before you allow them to use a sharp sword?"

"We do," Pharoah said. "Why do you ... ah, I know. The women need to use practice swords before they use sharp ones?"

"Yes," Xenia said, kissing Pharoah on the cheek. "You are so intelligent. We do not want to hurt each other —"

"Much," Egyptus murmured.

"— while we learn." Xenia turned to stare at Egyptus. "Why would we hurt each other at all?"

"We hurt each other to remind us to be watchful and never expect the enemy to do what we think they will do," Timor said. "You do not remember the bruises Pharoah came home with when he practiced with the sword."

"I did not know him then," Xenia said.

"And you did not see the bruises on our sons," Pharoah said. "They were too manly and proud to let you know of their bruises. They no longer needed their mama to kiss away the bruises. It happens when we practice."

Egyptus set her staff in the dirt and leaned on it, ready to enjoy the coming discussion.

"We will use our protecting pads," Xenia mumbled.

"Your what?" Timor asked, barking a short laugh.

"We hit each other too hard," Xenia said. "We decided to make and wear pads to protect our bodies."

"While I do not want to see bruises on Alma or any of you women, you will find the pads will get in your way and you will not learn as fast," Timor said, shaking his head. "We tried to use pads when learning to use the sword, but they are bulky and make it difficult to move."

"You will see," Xenia said, folding her arms in front of her.

"You will see," Timor agreed, smirking.

"We have wooden practice swords, but not enough for all the women and all the young men and older boys who need to practice."

"Can we trade times when we use them? Perhaps allow us to use them a span after sunrise, giving you a span to teach the boys. You can send them over for the women to use," Xenia asked.

Pharoah rubbed his chin in thought. "I suppose we can do that. The boys can run the wooden swords to you after they practice. I will have to ask Corom and Jakob to make more for us. They will be happy to travel into the forest for more wood."

"They will not go alone. They will take other men with them, will they not?" Egyptus asked. "We never know when or where our enemies will attack us."

Pharoah rolled his lips inward and sighed. "What happened to the safe, peaceful Egypt we discovered?"

Xenia and Egyptus glanced at each other.

"You know," Xenia said. "Those men who lost their families because they could no longer speak with them chose to attack us and make us as miserable as they are."

"You are correct. I know," Pharoah said, wrapping an arm around his wife. "But I miss our days of safety."

"We all do," Timor said, rattling the sword by his side. "What can we do to bring them back?"

He is ready to go back to sparring.

"I do not know, but we need to think and pray about that. Jehovah knows. He will help us discover the way," Pharoah said, bending to kiss Xenia. "Until then, we must practice and be ready for them when they return."

"If we include everyone in the considering," Egyptus said, still thinking of ways to prevent attacks by their enemies, "perhaps we will discover a way to solve this problem sooner. It is important to everyone in Egypt."

"I will bring it up in our next Sabbath meeting," Pharoah said. "But right now Timor and I have a sparring match to finish." He gently pushed Xenia back and drew his sword from its sheath. "You women should step out of the way."

"One more thing before you return to your sparring match," Egyptus said.

Each man dropped their arm holding a sword. Timor twisted toward his mama. "What more is there?"

"Ester suggested we learn how to fight with our belt knives. She is correct. We all carry our knives with us at all times. It is one weapon we always have with us."

"It is a bloody thing to fight up close with a knife," Pharoah warned.

"We know, but we want to learn to do it if we must. Also, we need to know how to throw our knife, like the boys do."

"You would lose your only knife," Timor said.

"Yes. But we plan to have a second one on our belt or in our shoe."

"Are there that many knives available?" Timor asked.

"I do not know," Egyptus said. "We will get them when we can. For now, would you assign us a young man or boy to teach us how to throw our knives, and a more experienced man to teach us to fight up close?"

Pharoah shuddered. "I would rather not, Mama."

She stared at him.

"But if you insist, I will. When do you want them to come?"

"Tomorrow morning."

He heaved a big sigh. She knew he could not argue with her.

"I will send a young man tomorrow morning."

"And the experienced man?" Egyptus pressed.

"Two days after. You do not want the women to have too much to think about. Now, we must complete our match."

Timor and Pharoah raised their swords in front of them to salute the women, then turned toward each other and resumed their match.

Xenia and Egyptus stood and observed their match, watching for the ways they each avoided hits and the moves they made.

"I will see you later," Egyptus said after watching for a time. "I need to report to the women."

Xenia nodded, engrossed in the men's movements. Egyptus wondered if the daughter of her heart even noticed her leaving.

~~

Iram surprised Egyputs and the other women when he showed up the next morning at their staff practice to help them learn how to throw their knives. Some women looked shocked that a young boy would come to teach them.

"You want to learn how to throw a knife?" Iram asked, ignoring the looks of consternation some of the young women gave him.

Lexa looked up at the sky.

"I have been throwing my belt knife almost since Papa gave it to me. It is something we boys do. We see who can throw it straighter, with more accuracy, and closest to the mark. I win almost every time I throw with my friends. That is why Papa sent me."

Ester stared at the ground, shaking her head.

Iram gazed at the younger women, then at the others. "I can teach you my secrets ... if you want."

Lexa and Ester glanced around the circle. Most of the women nodded their heads.

"What do we do first?" Alma asked.

Iram withdrew his belt knife from the sheath. "The first thing to remember is that you cannot hold your knife tightly if you need it in a hurry."

The women nodded and made encouraging noises.

"Take your knife out," Iram instructed. The women pulled knives from sheaths hanging from their belts. Over the next span, Iram showed them how to hold the knife and focus on the spot they wanted to hit. He gave them time to practice and went from woman to woman, giving them help and encouragement.

When Iram came to encourage Egyptus, she did her best to do what he had shown them. As he turned to move to another woman, she said, "I am proud of you, Iram. I did not know you had such skill with a knife. You are a kind and patient teacher. Thank you."

Red crept up the boy's neck and cheeks.

"Papa told me I had a talent and I should share it."

"You do. Now go help Isa."

Iram grinned at her and moved on to help Isa with her grip.

By the time Iram had helped every woman, they had spent more time than usual in their practice. Cira rushed away before he left, needing to feed her baby. At the end, the women hurried home together to feed their families their morning meal.

"You did well, Iram," Egyptus said.

"Did I, Grandmama?" he asked.

"You did. I hope you will return tomorrow to ensure we all are learning what we should."

"You should all practice and have competitions."

Egyptus nodded. She had been thinking the same thing.

Two days later, Arvad appeared in the middle of their staff practice.

"Pharoah sent me to teach you how to fight up close with your knife." He stared around the group of women whose faces had suddenly lost color. "I pray to Jehovah that you never need to use what I am about to teach you."

He showed them what to do and had them use sticks he had brought for them to practice with. "I do not want anyone hurting another while learning to do this," he said.

Using Magda to demonstrate, he showed them what to do if someone came too close.

"Aim your knife just below the center of his chest, below the bone that covers his heart."

"You will hit his lungs or some other important organ," Isa muttered. "Good place to stop a man."

"Yes, Isa is correct. We want him hurt enough he will not continue fighting."

He worked with the women until they could follow his directions and practice without shirking.

Before the practice session broke up, Arvad complemented the women for learning fast. "Like I said earlier, I pray you never need this skill. However, we do not know what our enemy will do next. It is smart of you women to prepare yourselves, even if you never need it."

In the next days, several men took a wagon and marched off into the forest to the northwest. Moren went with them, remembering a place that looked like it could contain the metal he would need for making swords.

While they were gone gathering wood for new practice swords, the men, boys, and women who stayed behind continued to practice each day with staffs, knives, and the shared wooden swords. Women took turns on the walkways watching for any possible attackers.

One afternoon, Eber, along with Kashet and Jov, brought a new design of his boat to Egyptus to see. "I think this one will float and carry us."

Carrying Buttercup in her arms, Egyptus hurried out her door to inspect the new boat. They had used the long reeds, cutting the inside away to make it more flexible, and woven it tightly together. It was only wide enough for one person, but long enough for two or three. The front and back rose to long thin points that would rise above the water almost half as high as Eber stood.

"That is a beautiful boat," Egyptus said. "Will it float?"

Buttercup leapt from her arms into the boat. She walked along its length before curling up in the front end.

"It looks like Buttercup thinks it will float," Egyptus said, reaching in to lift the cat out.

"She can ride along with us," Kashet said.

"She would not like to get wet," Egyptus argued, still leaning across the side of the boat.

"Leave her there," Eber said. "I have seen her swimming in the river. If she chooses not to ride in the boat, she can jump out before we put it in the water."

Egyptus sighed and stood up.

"We are going out to test it one more time," Kashet said. "Will you go with us?"

"Do you have your swords to protect us?"

Kashet and Eber patted the swords that dangled from their hips. "We do," Jov answered. A bandage was still wrapped around the injury he received during the last enemy attack. "We hoped you would bring your sword, too. Our uncles, Eber's papa, and our mamas are coming to watch and help protect us. But we need your sword."

"All those swords will protect you from the crocodiles, but I will get mine," Egyptus said with a laugh. She returned to her house to retrieve both her staff and sword from behind her door before she closed it. She tied the sword belt around her waist. "Lead the way. I am ready."

The three young men lifted the papyrus boat with the cat onto their shoulders and marched down the paths toward the gate. Several other men, women, and children followed them, laughing and shouting encouragement.

At the gate, Timor called up to those guarding from the walkway. "Is it safe to go to the river?"

"We see no one on the horizon, but we will watch closely," Jason replied. "If someone comes, we will warn you."

"Thank you," Egyptus said as Arvad opened the gate for the crowd to troop through.

They made their way to the riverbank. Buttercup woke and stood in the boat with her paws resting on the sides, gazing around at the scenery. It surprised Egyptus that she did not leap from the boat.

At the river's edge, the young men set their boat on the edge of the water with the front floating in the water.

"Say a prayer for us, please, Grandmama Egyptus," Jov said.

Everyone knelt near the boat while Egyptus led them in a prayer. "Jehovah, bless this boat and those who will ride in it." When she finished, those around her nodded and murmured an amen.

Jov, Eber, and Kashet climbed into the boat. Buttercup dropped out of sight.

"Where is my cat?" Egyptus asked.

"Curled up in the front again," Eber said.

The boys' papas pushed the rest of the boat into the water. Egyptus and others sucked in a breath as the boat bobbed near the shore.

It floated!

Kashet and Eber picked up oars they had made of lightweight wood and dipped them into the water, paddling away from the shore. The boat responded and as the young men wanted.

Everyone on the shore cheered while the young men rowed out to the center of the river. They let it carry them a distance downriver before they paddled back upriver toward their families and friends. They guided the boat to the shore and the men waded in to pull it out of the river.

Eber, Jov, and Kashet whooped with joy.

"We saw big fish out there!" Kashet cried.

"We need to take our fishing nets and baskets next time," Eber agreed.

"And spears," Jov added. "We need spears for the bigger fish."

"More food for us," Alma said.

"It would be nice to leave the boat here," Jov said, gazing longingly at the river.

"Not yet," Magda said. "Your papa will want to see your boat float. Although we know it floats and you will be safe, you never know when the enemy will come to attack us again. You would not want them to steal your efforts."

The excitement fell from Jov's face. He and his friends sighed.

"Where is my Buttercup? Did she leap out into the water to become crocodile food?" Egyptus asked.

Emer laughed. "Not your Buttercup. She leaned over to watch the fish, but she stayed inside where it is safe. She will be a good ... what do you call one who rides in a boat?"

"Seaman?" Timor asked.

"We are not going to the sea," Jov said. "Riverman works better. Buttercup makes a great river cat."

The three young men lifted the boat, cat and all, to their shoulders and carried it back within Egypt's protective walls.

Egyptus followed with the others, glancing into the distance where the enemy had often appeared. She did not see anyone.

No men attacked that day. However, Egyptus knew they would return. And she knew it would be difficult for the people of Egypt.

It did not take Jakob and Corom long to carve practice swords from the lengths of wood they had brought back from their expedition. Soon the women had enough swords they no longer needed to share for their daily practice.

Moren worked outside the village to heat and smelt the ores he found on the wood cutting trip.

"He will have to go back for more ore," Isa told Egyptus after an early morning practice. "He did not have enough space in the wagon to get all he will need to make all the required swords and knives. He suspects we will need more in time. He found an area with many of the ores he needs."

"Did he cover it so others would not find and take the ore?" Egyptus asked.

"He did. He says he first thought to leave it available for any who knows how to dig and smelt the ore. However, the impression came to him it would not be wise to leave the ore available for our enemies. Perhaps when they learn to trade, we can trade ores." A pained look filled Isa's face. "I do not like that he finds it necessary to return to that skill, even though I know it is necessary for our safety and survival. We prayed long and thoughtful prayers before he agreed to do this again."

"It is difficult to have to be ready to fight and kill our brothers. I would rather trade ores for other purposes than for weapons." Egyptus sighed and lifted her staff and started toward home.

Isa picked hers up and followed behind. "Trading ores is better than trading blows."

"It would be good to trade. We need the swords, but it would be better to trade with those men who think they must steal from us. If only they could settle down and have something to trade, rather than always trying to take from us."

The two women strode off the village green toward their homes.

"How will we get them to do that?" Isa asked.

Egyptus rubbed the back of her neck. "I do not know. All I know to do is to leave it in Jehovah's loving hands. He does not want us to be fighting and killing each other. He can help us get along."

"It would help if we could understand each other's words."

Egyptus nodded. "That is the big problem. It drives others away to different lands, but if we want to become friendly and trade with them, we need to communicate."

"Jehovah has His reasons for separating everyone. It is hard for us now. May it grow easier in the future," Isa said, bowing her head.

"Amen," Egyptus added. "May it be so."

They reached the point where their paths diverged to each of their homes.

Egyptus stopped. "We have to stop fighting. Someone from Egypt will die in the battles. If not the next one, it will be soon."

"Jehovah has blessed us to avoid death. Jov's arm was seriously injured in the last battle, as was Lim's leg. They are only now healed enough that I do not have to check on them daily."

"It is good they are almost healed. We will not always be so blessed. Our village is too small to lose our people to invaders. We must depend more on Jehovah and follow his laws more carefully."

"I have been preparing more healing remedies. If our enemies injure more of us, I will need someone to help me." She licked her lips. "I should teach someone to prepare the healing remedies and the principles of healing."

"Do you have someone in mind?"

"Not yet. I will watch the women and see who shows an interest. Some of the younger girls have hung around, wanting to know what I do. Maybe one of them."

"It may be easier to teach a younger girl not yet set in her ways."

"Yes. I have seen some who refuse my assistance because it is not what their mama would do."

"I know the one. Yes. A younger girl who is eager to learn is probably better. Is there one you are considering?" Egyptus scraped a line in the dirt at her feet with her staff.

"Xenia's daughter, Ami, is a smart girl. She asks smart questions and remembers the answers I give."

"She is intelligent. Perhaps you should speak to her parents about teaching her. Ami would be a talented healer. She has always been gentle and patient, especially with her younger brothers and sister."

"It would be best if I asked Pharoah and Xenia before I talk to Ami. I would not want to build up her hopes only to discover her parents are against it." Isa's staff scratched a line in the dirt crossing Egyptus's line. "She may want to be more like her grandmama. She always has a bit of papyrus and a pen in her pocket."

Egyptus smiled. "She does. She loves to write."

"She copies the instructions I give her for making a healing tea when I taught her to prepare it. She is smart enough to know not to always trust your memory." Isa scraped a circle around the scratches in the dirt.

"She knows what she wants. If she wants to learn to be a healer, her mama and papa cannot to stop her. I suggest you speak to them today." Egyptus sighed thinking of all the tasks that lay befor her. "I need more papyrus. There is always another young couple planning to marry. There are several who will decide soon. I need to make more scrolls of the Book of Commandments and have them set aside, so I am not rushing to finish one for them." She ran her staff through the design in the dirt.

"I have more tinctures to prepare and bandages to make and roll. I would rather have more than I need than not enough when sick or injured people come to my door." Isa lifted her staff. "I will see you later. Send Ami my way if you see her. I could use her help."

"Even if you have not spoken to her parents?" Egyptus lifted an eyebrow.

"I am not asking her to be my student today. I need her help. Maybe she has a friend who will come help too. There are never enough hands when I need to make large quantities of this tincture."

"If learning to heal keeps Ami away from the fighting, I would not mind. I would worry less for her," Egyptus said. "I will send her your way."

"She is a special girl."

"She is." Egyptus lifted her staff in salute and turned to stride toward her home.

Feigning Death

L ife in Egypt moved on peacefully for another month. In that time, men and women harvested the fields, while keeping their weapons close. Guards always stood on the walkways, watching for the enemy. The women continued to practice with their weapons, becoming more proficient with the new ones, and the men practiced shooting arrows and throwing spears. Pharoah changed some of their defense plans, fearing that Cain and Ludim would remember their fighting tactics and use it against them.

They had planned to plaster clay along the top of the walls, making them more difficult for the ropes to catch between them. However, they had not had time yet to dig the clay and begin the project.

Ami became Isa's student and came often to share her excitement with Egyptus. She gushed about the new things Isa taught her.

"I did not think Isa would teach me. I wanted to learn but did not think I could ask. Then Mama told me Isa needed a student and asked for me!" The girl wrapped her arms around herself. "I sometimes wake up wondering if it was all a dream."

"It is no dream. Isa spoke to me before speaking to your parents. She wanted someone who was interested, and you came often asking good questions and listened to her answers."

Later, as the village women set their last baskets of grains and their last squash into the storage sheds, the sound of a shell blasted through the valley. Egyptus glanced up, confused.

"That sounds like a bigger shell. Who got a bigger shell?" she asked.

"Kib picked up a shell on the beach the last time we went to gather salt," Rebecca said. "He has been practicing. Is there a problem?"

Chana shrugged. "We can only go to our newly assigned fighting assignments and be ready for them if it is the enemy."

Egyptus tied her sword in its scabbard around her waist, then grabbed her staff from where it leaned against the storage building and ran to the east wall of the village.

Pharoah had assigned her here as part of the new plan. Others in the group she fought with before continued to be in her group now. However, he had moved them from the back wall to the east wall. She still fought with Jason and Devora and Timor and Alma. Shez with Angetta, and Lim with Adara were now part of the group.

Additionally, Pharoah had assigned Jov and Kashet, who had fought well against the enemy outside the wall to their fighting group. He had assigned their friend Eber to another group. Esrom also fought with them as he had before, although his assignment was to be a message runner.

Timor led this smaller group. They had fewer women to fight with, but more men. Nyssa had attached herself to the group. Egyptus did not argue. The young woman had attended all the early morning practices since before the last attack. She had not developed her skills fully, but she would be an addition to the fighting group, as long as the enemy did not focus more than one man against her.

Now the men rushed up the stairs while the women gathered below.

"Is this real?" Angetta asked. "I have never heard them blow that horn as a warning before."

Shez turned from peering over the wall. He swallowed a few times in hesitation before speaking. "It is real. There must be fifty men racing toward us."

"How can you see that many? Are they not coming from the northwest toward the front gate as they did before?" Devora asked.

"Not this time. They come from the east and are running for our wall. They are not splitting up. I cannot see if more men are running toward the gate."

"Not splitting up?" Egyptus asked, the trickle of dread filling her stomach became a raging river engulfing her.

"No. They are all running toward our wall. Esrom, go tell Pharoah what is happening!"

Esrom started to argue, before he glanced out at the approaching men. He raced along the walkway toward the gate and Pharoah.

The sound of racing men slowed as they neared the wall. The thumping of ropes banged against the wall. Many hit against the wall below, but did not reach the top. However, enough ropes flew over the top that the five men assigned there struggled to throw them back down.

Jov and Kashet flung stones over the wall, hitting and causing many of the climbing men to lose their grips.

More ropes bumped against the wall. Some came over the top and caught between the logs. As before, some invaders avoided the falling rocks as they climbed up and into the village.

Timor and Shez continued to throw the flying ropes back over the side while Jason, Lim, and Kashet readied themselves to fight any man who peered over the top.

"Be ready," Egyptus called to the women in a low voice. "They will come for us."

The women readied their staffs. Those with swords loosened them in their scabbards. Egyptus hoped they had learned enough to fight and with the swords not hurt themselves.

Strange men climbed over the top of the wall. Timor, Jason, Shez and Baraq met them with swinging swords slashing and stabbing. With shouts of pain, the enemy fought against the swords. When injured enemy men fell from the walkway, women stepped forward to hit them with their staffs. Some tried to stand and fight, but the women moved quickly to beat them into submission. One or two men moved to grab a woman, but Egyptus and her women were ready, refusing to allow them to come near enough to catch them.

Shouting from above caught Egyptus's attention. Several men of Egypt joined in the battle on the walkway, fighting off the invaders. Grunting, they shoved as many as they could over the side and out of the village. Some stood firm and turned with drawn swords toward the men of Egypt.

Together, three intruders leapt from the walkway with a yell.

"Beware!" Egyptus shouted.

The women on the ground turned in time for each to swing her staff into an invader, slowing his momentum toward her.

Egyptus battered at her attacker, who met her swinging staff with his sword. She groaned and stooped and swung her staff in a low circle. The attacker jumped over the staff. She yipped and lifted it and allowed it to swing toward him again, at the level of his knees.

He could not leap over it. Instead, he stumbled with a yelp. Egyptus turned the staff and brought the tip up from the ground between his legs, into his groin.

He shrieked and dropped his sword. Egyptus jerked her staff back and walloped his chest. His eyes rolled upward and closed. He fell back, landing with a thud.

Egyptus glanced around to ensure the others were doing well. Other women had joined their group, and many more men lay at their feet. Each woman had overcome an enemy.

With a shout, another man leapt from the wall toward her. Alerted by the sound, she turned to meet his attack with her staff, pushing him away and trying to stay far enough back that his sword could not reach her. He dodged her swing, returning with a sword slash she barely caught on the side of her staff. She stabbed the staff toward his chest. He stepped aside.

She fought on. He evaded every move she made. She did not want to kill any of the men she fought, nor did she want them to touch her with their swords. That could end her fighting forever.

At last, she feinted a swing to his head. He ducked into the sweep of the staff she had suddenly lowered. He fell to the ground, unmoving.

She looked up for more.

At last, no more men fought with the women on the ground. The enemy on the walkway had been silenced as well. With a rapidly beating heart and weak legs, Egyptus gazed at the men lying around the women. A few groaned, but none tried to stand. Most were unconscious.

"How many did you fight?" Egyptus asked, brushing back hair from her face that had loosened in her exertion.

"I have no way of knowing," Alma said. Her face glowed red. Egyptus suspected hers did as well. "I did not count the men who attacked me."

"Nor did I," Nyssa said. Her usually neat hair had loosened and encircled her face in a disheveled mess. "Those men kept leaping off the edge of the walkway. All I could do was remember the fast practices Magda led and work as fast as I could to swing my staff at their head and knock them down."

"Good work," Angetta said, patting the young woman on the shoulder. Her skirt had torn during the battle. "That is all I could do. I did not have time to watch what others did. Too many men ran toward me."

"We would not have survived if these other women had not joined us. Five of us is not enough when there are this many men fighting against us," Egyptus said, panting still from the exertion. "Did all their men focus on our wall? It is good you women came to join us," Egyptus said.

Cira and Marji nodded.

"When our men ran toward your wall, we ran behind them," Bina said.

"If they did not, they had a gigantic force of men to attack one small village," Angetta said. "Even fifty men is more than we have. What do they want from us?"

"Food. Women. I suppose," Egyptus answered.

"Why would they attack us if they wanted us?" Nyssa asked.

"Perhaps they wanted to take us prisoner," Alma said.

"I am not willing to be any man's prisoner," Angetta said, stabbing the end of her staff into the ground.

Shez bounced down the stairs and wrapped an arm around her waist. "Good thing, I have no desire to lose you to any man, as prisoner or for any other purpose."

Angetta brushed a kiss across his lips. "Now what do we do?"

"Tie them up so they cannot continue to fight when they waken," Egyptus said. She retrieved the ropes kept beneath the walkways.

Angetta helped carry the ropes so they could tie up the prisoners. While Timor and Jason guarded them, the others tied their arms and legs.

"No need to tie this one," Baraq said. "He no longer lives."

"Nor this one," Shez said.

As they went from prisoner to prisoner, the men often called out that this prisoner had no need of binding.

"Are you certain we killed this many men?" Egyptus asked. "Is it possible they are feigning death?"

"Perhaps they are, but they seem to be dead," Shez said.

Egyptus crouched down and touched a man the others had declared dead. He felt warm to her. "Jov?"

"Yes, Grandmama?" he said, running to her.

"Would you please go find Isa? I know she is probably busy helping the injured, but I need her opinion. Please tell her this is important. Vitally important."

"Yes, Grandmama." Jov sprinted toward Isa's home.

"Jov!" Egyptus called.

The young man stopped running and turned back toward her. "Yes?"

"I believe she is helping the injured close to the gate."

Jov changed directions and dashed away.

"What makes you believe these men are feigning death?" Alma asked.

"This man is still warm. Even with this warm day, he should be cold." Egyptus took another rope and tied the man's arms.

A moan escaped from his lips.

"As I suspected," Egyptus said. "Not all these men are dead. I suggest we tie at least the arms of every man until we are certain he is truly dead."

"Such a horrible thing to think," Devora said as she reached into the pile of ropes for another to tie a man they had skipped.

"I am certain some of these men are dead," Timor said.

"Some," Egyptus agreed, stooping to tie the hands of another man. "But not all. They have some kind of sorcerer among them. That man," she motioned with her chin toward the man who had moaned, "is not dead, although he appears to be. Dead men do not moan."

Timor gulped. "Tie every prisoner's hands, even those you think are dead."

The small group of Egyptians grabbed more rope and bound each prisoner.

Isa hurried to the group. "Jov said you needed me."

"I do," Egyptus said. "Too many of our prisoners appear to be dead."

"Were you that vigorous in your fighting?" Isa asked.

"No, I think not. What made me wonder is that man." Egyptus waved toward to the one who had made a noise. "He is warmer than a dead man should be. When I tied his hands, he moaned. I fear a sorcerer has enchanted them."

"Or provided them with a potion, making them appear to be dead. Then they could revive and attack us from behind," Isa said with a small shudder. She turned, staring around the area. "Esrom!" she called.

"Yes, Isa?" Esrom said as he jogged over to them.

"Please run back to those who are tying up the prisoners on the green. Tell your papa I said to tie every man, even those he believes to be dead. I will tell him more when I return."

"Yes, Isa," Esrom said, rushing away to relay the message.

"There were many dead at the front gate as well?" Egyptus asked.

"I wondered at the numbers of dead. Some had no damage to their bodies that would kill them. Which of these are supposed to be dead?"

"The ones who only have their hands tied," Timor said.

"Not their feet?" Isa asked.

"If they are dead, even their hands will not matter," he said with a shrug.

"If they are alive, you will be sorry when they pull knives from their boots and cut their cords to attack us from behind," Isa said.

Egyptus cringed at the thought.

"I will tie their feet after you check to be certain all of them are dead," he said.

"You should," Isa agreed. "Even if they seem to be dead, they could waken. You should search them for hidden weapons, too, while they sleep."

Egyptus went with Isa as she examined each supposedly dead man. While Isa examined the man, Egyptus searched him, touching their bodies in places a woman would not normally touch a strange man.

"I am widowed, and these men look dead. It should not matter," she said with a shrug, although her stomach twisted as she searched.

Isa glanced at her and nodded. "They deserve it."

Jason and Baraq went through the men who were definitely alive and searched them for weapons. After they had searched all the men, they had a pile of knives laying off to the side.

More than one man shuddered as Egyptus searched his body for weapons, even though they appeared lifeless.

Kashet followed behind her and tied the legs of those who appeared to be dead after Isa completed her examinations.

"Now what?" Isa asked.

~~

In the end, all the men had weapons hidden on their bodies. They gathered one hundred knives and sixty swords from the prisoners or those killed.

They tossed all those who were dead, or supposedly dead, together in a pile away from the other prisoners.

"They stink," Pharoah had exclaimed, determined the other prisoners did not need to know of their suspicions.

They set the prisoners who had regained consciousness to digging a grave outside the walls. While they worked outside, guarded by men, other Egyptians guarded the pile of supposedly dead men. They could not know if or when the enchanted men would waken.

Later that afternoon, they had the prisoners drag the dead to the grave and ordered them to throw them into the hole, ties and all. Egyptus watched from the wall walkway.

How long before they wake from their enchantment and try to take us over? What will they do? They learned from the last attack. We will want to reconsider how we set up our fighting teams.

Even though they heard some groans and grunts, Pharoah ordered the prisoners to shovel dirt over the bodies.

One man suddenly dropped his shovel and stood with arms raised, shouting words at the other prisoners.

"You must bury them," Pharoah said.

"Ne! Ne!" the prisoners chanted.

"Why?" Pharoah asked.

The man who had raised his arms chattered in a language the people of Egypt could not understand.

Pharoah shook his head and ordered the men to shovel dirt onto the bodies again, using motions to show them.

The man, who seemed to be their leader, mimed men waking, stretching his arms above his head.

"No!" Pharoah said in a voice loud enough all could hear. He crossed his hands over his chest and closed his eyes. "Dead." Then he mimed shoveling dirt over them. "Cover them."

"Ne! Ne!" the man shouted. Once again, he acted like a man waking from a long sleep.

"As I thought," Isa said beside Egyptus. "Someone enchanted them to appear dead. These men knew and expected them to waken and attack us when we did not expect it."

"I suspected this as well," Egyptus said. "That man was too warm. He had not lost his water, either."

"Good symptoms of living. Some of those men are dead, but most are not."

"Why should I not bury those dead men? They stink." Pharoah asked again, holding his nose although he knew they were not all dead.

The leader ran from man to man in the pile of the dead, shaking them, trying to wake them. Some he shook once, then moved on to the next.

"He knows which are dead and which are enchanted," Isa said.

"It was their plan to attack us from within our walls," Egyptus said.

Slowly, the bound invaders stretched and tried to sit, then started yelling when they could not move.

The leader pointed at the moving men.

"Yes. They live, but you tried to make us think they were dead," Pharoah said, crossing his hands and brushing them outward.

The leader shouted and ran to untie one man in the grave.

"No!" Pharoah shouted. "Ne!" He used the same word the enemy had yelled.

Pharoah had planned for this. Three of his guards ran out and stopped the man. They pushed the prisoners who were to cover the bodies into a group and their arms tied again behind their backs. Then they dragged those who had "awoken" from the grave and threw them together with the other prisoners.

"What is Pharoah going to do with all these men? We have no place to lock up so many," Isa asked waving her hand toward them.

"I do not know. We will have to watch. He has been talking with the other men. He has a plan," Egyptus said. "But I think it changed when these men pretended to be dead. They should gag the men so they cannot speak to each other. It would make it harder for them to change plans." She leaned on the wall, gazing out at the prisoners.

"And harder for them to breathe and eat."

Egyptus turned toward her friend. "I do not trust them. There is no safe place to put them for the night. They deserve to spend the night in the open, with the wild animals."

"But do our men deserve to stand in the night to keep the prisoners from breaking out to attack us again?" Isa asked.

"That is the problem. It is good Pharoah is the one responsible to determine their doom, not me. I would tie their hands and feet together and leave them out in the cold."

"We gained many more swords from this encounter," Isa said. "We now have enough swords for all our women and younger sons."

"And knives. We could all have an extra or two. How is Moren doing with his ore smelting?" Egyptus asked.

"He is working on it, but the ore he found is not as pure as that of Shinar. That makes Moren work longer to smelt it. It helps we took more swords in this battle. He will have less pressure to make new swords and knives. He would rather make more useful things than swords to hurt and kill others."

"We would all prefer to live and get along with our neighbors."

"Do you think we can do that before these little ones are old enough to stand up in battle against our enemies?"

"I hope we can protect more of this valley soon. We need to live on our lands away from this small village. I do not know how we can do that soon, but we must try," Egyptus said standing and turning her back to the prisoners below. "We must call on Jehovah and ask for his help with this and our other problems."

Plans

P haroah did not plan to keep the enemy within the walls of Egypt through the night. Instead, he had the women bind sticky papyrus around their eyes and herded them, almost like cattle, out across the wilderness away from the village, with their hands still tied behind their backs.

"He did not even give them the benefit of a ride," Gilit complained to whomever would listen as they drew water from the well two mornings later.

"Why would you care?" Angetta asked. "They are our enemy and tried to kill us."

"Did you know that?" Egyptus asked, standing in the shade of a big sycamore fig, waiting for her turn to get water. "Did you join your fighting group to fight them off?"

"No. I do not fight. I am a woman, and women do not fight!" Gilit said, drawing herself up to her full height. "It is unseemly to see women fight against men."

"You would rather they take you as their prisoner than fight them?" Egyptus asked, her amazement caused the water pouring water from the bucket into her urn to stop briefly.

A cloud crossed the sun, dimming the light for a breath.

"No. But Animim and our sons should protect me," Gilit said in a pouting voice. "They do not. They go off elsewhere, rather than stay near me. I hide in ..."

Egyptus glanced toward her in time to see her glance furtively around.

"Well, I hide. You do not need to know where," Gilit finished.

"You allow everyone else to fight battles to protect you while you hide?" Magda asked. "The young women gather with the babies and little children in the sanctuary, but even they are prepared to fight off the enemy to protect the children. And you hide?" Disdain dripped through her words.

Egyptus wanted to cheer. It was good to hear someone else express the thoughts she forced herself to repress as leader of the women.

The small cloud blew away from the sun, brightening the day once more.

Gilit stood straighter. Egyptus wondered how she could do that.

"I am a daughter of Shem. We are protected. We do not fight." Gilit lifted her urn of water to her shoulder and stalked away toward her home.

"She thinks she is special," Angetta spat out after Gilit had disappeared around a corner. "She is no more special than any of the rest of us."

"She is lazy, not special," Hibah said, moving to take a turn at the well. "She has always been like this. Even in Shinar. When there is anything she does not want to do, she uses that tired excuse of being a daughter of Shem."

"Why did she come with us, then?" Magda asked. She stepped over to help Hibah draw the bucket up.

"I can do this," Hibah said. "I am not a lazy daughter of Shem."

"Who is your papa?" Angetta asked. "I do not think I have ever heard."

Egyptus leaned back to gaze into the tall tree. The figs would be ripe and fall in a few days. They would add it to their food supply.

Hibah pulled on the rope. "My papa? My papa is Shem. Gilit is my sister, although I only claim her when I must. She came with us for the same reason I did. We wanted to be with our children who married Afra's and Egyptus's children. When they told us of your plight, that Niva and her gang of women attacked and would attack again, we knew we must join you or never see those children again."

"But you have other children," Egyptus said. "You will never see them again." A dark cloud sent a shiver up her spine.

"One son has come to Egypt as an enemy." Hibah allowed her long hair to fall across her face, hiding it. "The man Pharoah called Cain. That was my son. No longer. He fell from Jehovah's grace when he attacked us."

Soft gasps escaped from the women's lips.

"You cannot believe there is no longer hope for him!" Egyptus cried, chasing away the dark cloud in her heart.

"No. I pray for him every day. However, until he sees the light of Jehovah's love once more, he is not my son."

Women gathered around Hibah, taking turns hugging her.

"It is a burden I carry," Hibah said at last. "Gilit is my older sister. Cain was my son."

"Cain is not the name you gave him. What did you call him?" Egyptus asked. "Now I know why he looked so familiar to me."

"We named him Chanan. Cain fits him better now."

"Now I remember him. Chanan. He was compassionate as a young man," Egyptus said, giving Hibah a quick hug around the waist.

"He was. But like so many, Nimrod enticed him ... and we lost him."

Hibah moved away from the well, giving the next woman space to draw water.

"Nimrod. That man. Many of us older women have that story to tell," Isa said, sitting by Egyptus while she waited for her turn at the well. "I, too, lost a son to Nimrod."

Magda dropped the bucket into the well. When it splashed, she pulled on the rope to bring it back up. "Your stories are sad. I hope none of my sons follow evil men. It is good Nimrod is not here."

"But men change. Nimrod was not always bad," Egyptus said.

"We may yet see one of our sons forget Jehovah and become like Nimrod," Hibah said.

"We can hope they read and remember the words of the Book of Commandments you created for each of us," Magda murmured.

"It could happen," Alma said. "I pray it is not one of my sons. I do not know if I could live through that."

"Your sons are good and kind men," Egyptus said. "I doubt they will forget Jehovah. But if they do, you and I will remember and pray for them."

"We will all pray for our sons," Isa said.

When everyone had water in their urns and there was little left to say, the women made their way back to their homes. Egyptus carried her urn as she walked beside Xenia.

"How is Ami doing with Isa?"

"She chirps about this herb and that solution until she sounds like one of the little birds outside our window. She is happy." Xenia glanced down and stared at her feet. "But I miss her. She is gone more than I expected."

"There is much for her to learn. It is better she is there learning to heal than with us learning to kill with a sword or knife."

"She may still need those skills. Isa joins us most mornings."

"As does Ami. She will know how to defend herself if she must. I like that as a healer, her papa will not send her to a wall to protect it. Better to be with Isa, helping the injured."

"True. And she is happy learning." Xenia lifted a shoulder. "I miss her, though."

"As do I," Egyptus said as they parted.

With the fields and her garden harvested, Egyptus no longer needed to have Adok pour water into her garden furrows. She set her urn on the step by her back door and strode to her garden, wondering how the little rivulets had fared.

She bent to look at the furrows she and Adok had dug. The soil had built up along the sides.

Egyptus returned for her urn and spilled water into the furrow. Water flowed down the furrow, held back by the built-up sides.

"That is what we can do to hold the water back," she murmured. "But how tall will the walls have to be to keep the water out of our homes? Can we dig rivulets from the river to the fields to help divert the floods?"

She shook her head and carried her urn into her home with thoughts spinning in her head. Perhaps they could use bricks like they had used in Shinar. Bricks and earth could hold back enough water to protect their homes if they were far enough from the edge of the river. They could dig deep furrows from the river to the fields to water and absorb the floods.

She strode out her front door to search for Pharoah.

"He is not here today," Xenia said when Egyptus knocked on her door. "He is meeting with the men to discuss a way to better protect our community. Most of our people want to move out to their own land when the next floods recede."

"If they do, they will be at risk from our enemies who regularly attack us," Egyptus said.

"Yes. That is why they are meeting," Xenia said. "They need to make plans before people move out into the valley."

Egyptus nodded. "I hope they can resolve the problem. I know Isa would be happier if she could plant her herbs on her land and not fear the floods. We need to protect everyone's land from the floods."

"That is something Pharoah worries about."

"I may have a solution to that problem. I wanted to share it with Pharaoh."

"I will send him to you when he returns," Xenia said. "He will be happy to hear a solution to even one of our challenges."

Egyptus returned to her home, picked up her pen, dipped it into the ink, and doodled on a scrap of papyrus. She drew a rough outline of the land around the walls of Egypt, drawing in the lines of the river and its spreading fingers as it flowed closer to the Siddim. She added the fields and drew lines to show where she thought they could dig furrows from the river to the fields.

Buttercup entered the room and jumped onto her lap. Egyptus absently stroked the cat as she contemplated her sketch.

Why have we not dug these small river extensions to the fields before? I remember Eve and Adam did this soon after settling into Home Valley. We forget the good things our early parents did.

She drew lines along the edges of the river, marking where she thought the brick and mud walls should go to hold back the floods.

She made openings in the wall.

We need to pass through these walls. Maybe not a hole, but steps.

She rubbed away the openings and filled them in, drawing three lines on each side to indicate steps.

She continued sketching walls around the lands her family had chosen, trying to protect the land from floods.

"Are you here, Mama?" Pharoah asked as he opened the door.

"I am here," she said from her table.

"I knocked, but you did not hear." He joined her at the table. "What are you doing that you were so absorbed in your thoughts?"

Egyptus moved suddenly to show him her sketching. Buttercup yowled and jumped off her lap.

"I am sorry, Buttercup. I forgot you were there," she said.

She explained the new furrows they would dig to help flood the fields and the walls that would hold it back near the village and around the lands claimed by people when they first entered the valley.

"I like this plan," Pharoah said. He traced his finger along the river near Egypt. "But Eber will want a place to put his boats into the water. We will want to get past these walls to fish, gather papyrus, and dig clay. How will they get past these walls?"

"I thought steps on each side for people and animals to climb would work."

"It may help to put the walls closer to the hills and our fields where the floods initially rush into the valley. We may want to give the water space to spread out there and control it more when it gets closer to our lands," Pharoah suggested. "What gave you this idea?"

"Adok and I made tiny rivulets in my garden to get the water through it easier when I came back from the hills during the hottest time of the year. I went out to examine those furrows today and saw walls had built up along the edges of the rivulets holding back the water."

Pharoah set a hand on her arm. "I knew you could solve this problem. It may take more thought and some experimenting, but this is a great beginning."

"It will be a big job to make all the bricks that water will not wash away. People will wonder if we are trying to be like those who built the tower."

"No, Mama. We are not building a tower. We will use bricks to protect us. We should pray together about this. It is best we have Jehovah's support. I will share with the others during our next Sabbath day."

~~

During the next Sabbath meeting, Pharoah spoke about the concerns everyone had about the coming floods. He had taken Egyptus's doodles and walked along the land, checking to be certain they matched. Then he had enlarged the map onto a larger piece of papyrus, big enough for all to see the markings.

"We are thinking of some easier ways to water our gardens and fields and protect our homes from the flood." Pharoah unrolled the enlarged map for all to see.

"If we dig canals from the river to the fields, they will have sufficient water to grow bigger and better crops."

"What do we do to stop the water when we no longer need it to be soaking our fields?" Akish asked.

"That is easy," Jakob said. At Pharoah's nod, he stood and walked to the front. "I remember seeing this used in Shinar. They placed a dam at the beginning of the canal. When they needed water, they removed the dam or turned it to allow only a portion of the canal to be filled with water."

"What do we do during the floods? The water will overflow our dams," Lim asked.

"We remove the dams and allow the floods to cover our fields. The rich mud the floods bring gives life to our soil," Jakob said.

"That is a lot of work," Chayim said.

"Less work than carrying buckets of water to the fields when the rains do not fall," Moren said. "It will take time and work, but it will be better for all of us in the end."

"That sounds good," Arvad said. "What are those other lines running along the edge of the river?"

"We hope that walls set away from the river a distance will hold back the floods and protect our homes and lands," Pharoah said. "I would like to try first with walls around Moren's and Isa's land. Her herbs and other healing plants help keep us healthy and alive."

"My plants would appreciate growing in only one place. They do not like to be dug up and replanted twice every year," Isa said.

The crowd in the sanctuary murmured their agreement. Many had helped dig and move Isa's plants before and after the flood season. None spoke words of dissent.

"Can some others of us have these walls around our property?" Shule asked.

"We will extend the walls to surround each of your lands as soon as we can. They will require many bricks to build these walls. But first, we will want to extend the walls up the river part way to keep the floods away from our homes here in our walled village. We hope it will make it possible for you to have homes all along the Black River," Pharoah said.

"Who is this 'we' you speak of?" Gilit asked.

"My mama has been trying to solve this problem for many weeks, many years, since our first flood. This is her solution."

"Would it not make the floods higher if we walled them closer to the hills?" Animim asked. "I have noticed that the water builds up when contained in a narrow channel."

"It would," Pharoah said.

"But this is Egyptus's plan," Gilit said, standing. Hatred twisted her face. "Why is it you always use her plans?"

Heads swiveled to stare at Gilit.

"Do you have a plan you think would work?" Pharoah stared pointedly at the older woman.

"No. But I might if I thought about it," she said.

"If you do, we will be happy to consider your plan," Pharoah said. He turned from her to the others in the room. "For now, no one else has offered another plan. I do not know if anyone else has been searching for a solution."

"It is easy to complain about a problem, more difficult to find a solution," Chana mumbled.

Laughter rumbled through the room, helping the frustration to dissipate.

Gilit sat straighter, unwilling to admit she recognized the laughter pointed in her direction.

"This is a problem we have dealt with since the first year of floods. Anyone is welcome to consider and share any ideas and plans you have. We must work together to solve our problems." Pharoah gazed around the room. He nodded to a group of boys. "Look at Emer, Kashet, and Jov and their boat. They did not wait for someone else to solve the problem."

Egyptians in the room buzzed for a short time as they discussed the solution Pharoah presented.

"I have a question," Corom said, standing.

"What is it?" Pharoah turned to his younger brother.

"How will you make the bricks that will form these walls? Mud will wash away, especially in the floods. Wood does not hold the water back well. We learned that in the high floods this year."

"I thought we would try making bricks similar to those they made in Shinar," Pharoah said.

"Bricks? Like the ones they used to build the tower?" Alma asked. "Is that safe?"

"The people who made those bricks worked to make them resistant to water," Pharoah replied. "I watched them make those bricks along the edge of our stream back in Shinar."

"But they went against Jehovah. Will we?" Alma asked once more.

"No. We are working to protect our lands, not to defy Jehovah's laws."

"What did they do to keep the water out?" Lexa asked. "I remember seeing wagons filled with the bricks, but I never saw them making them."

"They used mud filled with clay, and added sand and straw," Magda said. "I watched them, too. They let them dry before standing them on their edge and taking them away."

"I think they allowed them to dry for more than a week in the hot sun before they used them," Shiblom added. He shrugged when Tama looked up at him. "No. I did not help them make their bricks or build their tower. But I was curious to see how they made their bricks. Since they made them along our stream, I watched."

"Without asking permission to use our clay," Egyptus added. "I suppose it is no longer a problem for us. We no longer live on the Plains of Shinar and few of them do, either. Most of them were scattered."

After a long discussion, the people agreed they needed to make bricks, hoping they would help protect their homes from the ravaging damage of the river during the floods.

Some men agreed to dig canals from the fields to the Black River. Egyptus joined those willing to make the bricks.

"I can help with the bricks too," Isa said, "since we will put some of them at the base of the land Moren and I claimed. My healing plants will appreciate not having to be uprooted ahead of the floods."

"You will trust the walls?" Gilit asked.

Isa stared at the woman. "I trust Egyptus has tested her idea enough that it will work. Even if it does not work as she envisions, it will be better than not having any protection."

"How will you get to your land to care for those plants during the floods?" Emer asked.

"I will ask Eber, Jov, and Kashet to take me in their new boat," Isa said. Women in the room gasped.

"I saw their last effort. It floated down the river and back. Soon they will each have a boat to take out on the river to fish."

Voices raised in exclamations of joy.

"We will soon have many boats for fishing," Jov said. "We have found some of the best islands of papyrus grow down the river where the water is deeper. We cut papyrus from there and brought it home to use for our next boat."

"Others may want to ride along to fish or cut papyrus," Kashet said. "You would be welcome."

"Is your boat safe enough for that?" Hibah asked.

"Yes, Grandmama Hibah," Eber said. "We have been out on the river several times now. Not even the crocodiles can tip us over, as they did when we first started paddling on the river."

"Paddle?" Shule asked.

"We use paddles to help us move upriver and take us where we want to go," Jov answered. "Paddles are long sticks, wide at one end. We have used palm fronds, but they are not always easy to find. We made some especially for paddling."

"Congratulations to these young men," Pharoah said. "They saw a need and worked to resolve the problems around it."

"The only problem left is a safe place on the river to leave our boat," Kashet said. "We fear the enemies who attack our city will steal our boat, even if they do not know how to control it."

"That is a problem," Akish agreed. "I would suggest you leave it tied to a rock or bush on the shore —"

"But serpents and other creatures will find it and curl inside to sleep. That is not a good choice," Angetta said with a shiver.

"You can make a cover to keep the creatures out," Ada suggested.

"That is an excellent suggestion," Eber said. "But the bigger problem of those who come to attack our village stealing our boat still remains. We could tie it up, but the enemy can untie the knot or cut it."

"We will have to consider the problem," Timor said. "Until we find a reasonable solution, I suggest you bring it inside the village each time after you go paddling."

"The water makes it heavy, but we carry it inside now," Eber said. "We are searching for a better solution."

"I recommend everyone seeks to solve your challenges as Eber, Jov, and Kashet have," Pharoah said. "And my mama. If no one considers solutions to our problems, we will never solve them."

He stared out at the members of the village, lingering on Gilit. "We still have some concerns about where to place a wall to stop the flooding, but we can make bricks and dig canals to water the fields. While we do that, I ask that each of you plead with Jehovah for guidance about where to place the wall. Each of you has the right to receive that answer."

Women around Egyptus murmured to each other.

"Is that what you do, Egyptus?" Chana asked. "You always seem to find a solution to our difficulties."

"I pray morning and night, and many times in between," Egyptus said. "And I always include a request for assistance with the current challenge."

"We should follow Mama Egyptus's example," Pharoah said. "We should remember to pray night and morning and whenever we need help. Jehovah will help the faithful."

When the meeting ended and the villagers stood to leave the sanctuary, several women gathered around Egyptus.

"How did you know to dig canals?" one asked.

"How did you know to build a wall?" another asked.

"How did you know to ...?" others asked about other solutions Egyptus had offered in the time since they came to Egypt.

"I prayed and asked for Jehovah's help. Then I listened for the answer," Egyptus gave the same answer to each question.

"You listened?" Cira asked. "How?"

"I wait on my knees until I know Jehovah has heard, then I spend the day or night thinking of how I might solve the problem. This problem of controlling the river has been on my mind since the first flood. I have been patient."

"Patience," Lexa said. "That is something I am still learning."

"You will learn it more when you have your first child," Rebecca said, cradling her little daughter in her arms.

"Children have a way of teaching you patience," Hibah agreed.

"Listen patiently and do not give up. Jehovah will always answer our prayers and give us the assistance we need," Egyptus said.

Protection

In the following days, many men worked to dig canals from the fields to the Black River. They left the last short distance between the river and the canals solid, without digging it to keep the river from pouring down the canals.

Egyptus joined the other men and women mixing clay filled with soil, sand, and straw. They dumped the mixture into wooden brick molds and let it dry. They created many bricks, knowing they would need many more before the floods came.

She went with the others when they filled a wagon and carted blocks to Moren's and Isa's land. Many helped to stack the blocks, then smooth a mud slurry over them to make them smooth.

Before the rains came, they had completed the wall around Moren's and Isa's land, hoping to protect it. They had built other walls near the river and close to the village.

Each morning, men and women began their day practicing with their new weapons. The women soon learned that although pads helped protect them from bruising, they could not move easily in them. They soon left the pads home.

Canals were dug to all the fields, including opening them up and watching the water flow in. Jakob had shown them how to make dams to keep the water back until they needed it. The ease of watering the newly planted fields amazed the men. They hoped to grow another crop of grains before the floods.

Jakob suggested they plan to remove the dams when the rains came and replace them after the floods when they needed to water again.

"There is no need to put them in for the floods to wash them away," he had said.

Egyptus continued to work with those who made bricks. They lay them a distance from the river on the village side only, wanting to direct the flooding water across the land on the other side.

When clouds gathered above them, threatening to bring the yearly rains, they had built much of the planned wall. Egyptus watched the clouds, waiting to see if the brick walls would work.

When the rain fell on Egypt and dark, black thunderclouds hung in the distance to the south, Jakob and other men ran to remove the dams from the ends of the canals leading to the fields. They returned just before the rain fell.

Egyptus watched later that day from the walkway as the floods pushed trees and debris down the Black River.

Animals caught up in the flood climbed and raced across the land. Egyptus and others went out, as they had in the years before, to help free those that could live and harvest those that could not.

By the end of the second day, the flood water washed against the bottom of the low wall but did not overflow it. Instead, it spread out across the land on the other side of the river.

Egyptus breathed a deep sigh of relief. The wall held. For now.

"Did you bring your plants to your garden here?" Egyptus asked Isa, who also watched with her from the walkway.

"No. I said I trusted Jehovah and your wall to protect my plants. I cut some and brought them with me when we returned to the village. I fear we will need medicinal remedies during this raining season." Isa leaned forward against the wall.

"Do you expect illness?" Egyptus asked.

"I have seen illness in raining times like these. I am prepared for it when it comes."

"And for any injuries we may have if our enemies attack?" Egyptus turned her back to the flood and leaned against the wall.

Isa chewed on her lower lip. "We have been many months without an attack. Do you think the enemy will attack us in the rain?"

"Perhaps not in the rain, but they often come after we harvest our fields. It would be nice if they would come and ask to trade rather than always trying to take what is not theirs."

"It will happen one day," Isa said. "We face angry men who forgot Jehovah. There will come a time when they are no longer angry. They will band together and seek trade."

"We cannot expect the big cats to come protect us as they did last year," Egyptus said.

"Why?"

"It would be too much to expect from Jehovah to send us another miracle like that." Egyptus turned and stared down at the flood. "One thing I hoped for, but did not expect, is that the water is not lapping against our walls yet."

"That is good. We will not need to fear our homes flooding. We can pray and hope the water stays away."

"Good and bad. Our enemy can come closer to our walls and attack. We no longer have the protection of the floods." Egyptus gazed out at the land beside the river wall. Although it was soaking wet from the rain, no water protected them from their enemy.

"We face the enemy because we have protected our homes from the floods," Pharoah said, coming down the walkway to stand with Egyptus and Isa.

"Should we have allowed the floods to rise to the village walls?" Egyptus asked.

"No. This year everyone is still here inside. We can protect ourselves from an enemy together. When we scatter across our land it will be much harder to protect ourselves and our people," Pharoah said.

"What will we do?" Isa asked.

"I do not know. Jehovah will provide a way. He always does."

While the Black River flooded, no strangers came to attack Egypt. Egyptus and others stayed busy because Jov and Nyssa had announced plans to be married.

Egyptus wrapped a copy of the Book of Commandments she had copied during the year before and set it in a tall jar she had made and set aside to be given as a wedding gift.

Nyssa's mama and sisters had decorated the room beautifully with dried jasmine and roses that spread their fragrance within the room.

At the marriage rite, Egyptus sat with Ada, Nyssa's mama. "She is a beautiful girl. What does she think about Jov's boat?"

"They went out on the river together yesterday," Ada said. "I feared the whole time they were on the water. What if tree branches rushing deep down the river in the floods suddenly appear?"

"Our young believe they will not be injured. I remember the days when I believed that." Egyptus shook her head. "Not anymore."

The young couple joined their hands and listened to the sacred words Pharoah spoke as he married them. Ada leaned against Meyer. As often happened, Egyptus remembered the day Noah had joined her to Afra. They had knelt in front of Grandpapa Noah clasping hands as he said the sacred words.

Tears leaked from her eyes. She missed her beloved Afra. She wiped away the stray tears with her hand and smiled, hoping no one had seen.

Later, when she stood in line waiting to congratulate the young couple, Rebecca joined her. "You miss Papa today."

Egyptus turned sharply to stare at her daughter.

"I saw you wipe away tears. You only tear up when you miss Papa."

Egyptus allowed the breath she held to release. "Yes. I often do at these weddings. I thought about the day we were married. Noah spoke almost the same words to us. I miss him." They took steps forward, then stopped, waiting for the line to move again.

"Who? Papa?"

"Yes, your papa and my love, Afra. But I also miss my mama and papa, and Noah and Imma. Some days I feel so alone."

"But Mama," Rebecca cried, "we are all here with you."

"Some days I feel alone in a crowd. My husband is gone. I left my parents and the others of my generation. Everyone here has a mate. Everyone but me."

As they stepped forward again, Rebecca asked. "Would you take another husband if another man were available?"

Egyptus thought about it for a breath. "No. Even though I am lonely, I do not want another man in my life. I still have Afra."

The line moved and now Egyptus stood in front of the new couple. "Nyssa, you are glowing," she said. "And Jov, you have a beautiful wife."

"And I have an intelligent husband," Nyssa said. "Who else would have thought about building a boat to travel on the river?"

"I worked on it with Eber and Kashet. If not us, others would have thought about it," Jov said, his face coloring pink.

"Others may have thought about it," Egyptus said, "but what is important is that you did something with your thoughts. You built a boat that floats on the Black River."

"I had help," Jov said, clinging to Nyssa's hand.

"And with that help, you created something not used here before," Egyptus said. "Congratulations to both of you. You will be happy together as long as you remember Jehovah."

"It is with Jehovah's help that we are together," Nyssa murmured.

Egyptus smiled. "You will have to tell me that story sometime, but not today. Others are waiting to congratulate you."

She walked into the crowd of family and friends, speaking to most as she passed. Still, the sense of loneliness filled her.

Afra, why did you leave me?

A soft breeze passed her face.

'I did not leave you. I am here,' Afra whispered in her ear. 'Do not feel lonely.'

I am not lonely. I miss you.

Egyptus knew he would recognize her lie, but she thought it anyway.

No. I am lonely because you are gone.

'I know. I am here for you. All will be well.'

A gentle touch graced her face, then the breeze left.

"Mama?" Hulda said. "You look like someone kissed you."

"Someone did," Egyptus replied.

"But I did not see anyone near you." Hulda glanced around, seeking the one who had the temerity to kiss her mama.

"No. You will not see him. Your papa reminded me he is here with me."

"You look happier too."

"I am. I can survive this place with my children and be happy. I will be with my love someday. Until then, he watches over me."

Hulda shook her head. "Your trust and love are greater than mine. I would want another man."

"Where do you suggest I find one? None of the men here of my age are available, and I would not have a man who attacks us. Most of them are much too young, anyway."

"My brothers and sisters and I. We worry that you spend too much time alone." Hulda shrugged.

"You and who else?" Egyptus gazed around the room, then returned to stare at her daughter.

"It appears to everyone else that I am alone, but I spend much of my time with children and grandchildren."

"Mama. You have no man to stand beside you, to protect you, to keep you warm at night!"

Egyptus lifted her lips in a small smile. "No. No man keeps me warm at night, but Buttercup warms my feet when they are cold. Do you know anyone who wants one of her kittens? They do a good job keeping mice and other vermin out of the house."

"Buttercup has kittens again?" Hulda cried. "She is a prolific mama."

"She is. Do you want one?"

"Do not tell Jon! He will insist we get one."

"You need one to keep your feet warm."

"My Akish does that, thank you."

Perhaps Jov and Nyssa will want one," Egyptus mused.

"Do not ask them now! They have other things to think about," Hulda said.

"Like keeping their feet warm?"

Hulda tipped her head back and guffawed. "Mama, you make me laugh."

Egyptus often remembered the kiss she received from Afra that day. She would put her hand to her cheek to hold it there and remember. Afra could not be seen or heard by the others, but he protected her.

Traders

In time, the flood receded, leaving dark and fertile mud across Egypt's fields. Jakob and his sons set dams in the mouths of each canal leading to the fields so the land would dry enough to plant.

Before the fields had dried enough to plant, Egyptus worked in her garden, planting new seeds and making new furrows.

The sound she hoped to never hear again rang through the village. Someone blew on the shell, sounding the warning. Strangers, perhaps the enemy, were coming again.

She wrapped her sword belt around her waist, hoping not to need it, then grabbed her staff from where it leaned against the house before running out toward her assigned position near the front gate.

Pharoah had been concerned that the enemy had focused their latest attacks on the back and sides of the village where she had been assigned. He had moved her to the front where more people would be available to help protect her. Egyptus had argued that her groups needed her elsewhere. In the end, she had accepted his direction as leader of Egypt.

"What is happening?" she called up to Baraq, who stood as guard on the walkway near the gate.

"Men are coming," he said.

"Enemies?"

"All the others have been enemies," he said with a shrug. "We will have to see what these men do. Our men are rushing back to the village from the fields. I hope they get here before the strangers do."

Pharoah ran up the stairs and stared out at the coming men. "They are not waving weapons nor running. Could it be they come as friends?"

"When have strangers wanted to be friends?" Chayim said, joining Egyptus at the base of the stairs. "I remember that first time strangers came. It hurt." He rubbed the spot on his arm where the poisoned knife had injured him.

"You came close to dying that day," Isa said as she joined Egyptus and Chayim.

"I am here only because of your gifted healing," Chayim said. "You have kept me alive many times when I should have died."

Isa grinned. "Do not forget that. Show your gratitude by missing their arrows and swords today. Do not get hurt this time. Cira still needs you."

"And so do your babies," Egyptus added.

Chayim rushed up the stairs to go see what was coming.

"Let us know what you see," Isa called after him.

"Yes, Isa." His voice drifted back to them as he hurried down the walkway.

He's a good boy," Isa said.

"And a great papa," Egyptus agreed.

Families streamed through the gate. Women took their little ones to the sanctuary for safety, then joined the men rushing to join their fighting groups before the strangers arrived.

After a short time, Shem raced down the stairs, three at a time. "They have weapons, but they left them behind and are walking toward us with hands raised. It looks like they want peace."

"Do you really think so?" Isa asked, but Chayim had raced up the stairs as he had as a younger man.

"Still a boy," Egyptus said with a grin. "I hope they want peace, but I fear it is a trap."

"I do as well," Pharoah said, descending the stairs more sedately. "Their leader is asking for a meeting. I will go meet with him, but I do not trust him yet."

"How will you stay safe?" Egyptus asked.

"Animim and Akish are going with me. They will take their swords. I have men on the walkway with bows. If these strangers betray the peace, our men will shoot them."

Xenia hurried to join the small group. "Please be safe. We need you. I need you safe."

Pharoah embraced and kissed his wife. When they separated, he murmured, "You know I will be careful. I want to be here when —"

"Do not say that," Xenia said with a growl.

"I know. But I need to be here with you and our children. I will be careful. We prayed for protection this morning. Jehovah will protect me."

Xenia reluctantly allowed him to step from her arms. Egyptus put an arm around the daughter of her heart. "I will stand here with you. I am ready to fight them if they cheat."

The gate opened only wide enough for Pharoah, Animim, and Akish to slip through it. The men inside pulled the gate closed behind them, standing ready to open it quickly if the three men needed to enter fast.

Isa moved to the other side of Xenia and put her arm around her. "We are here for you."

The women stood still, listening for any indication the strangers were there to betray the trust Pharoah had put in them. All the Egyptians desired this peace.

Voices rose and fell from the other side of the wall. Egyptus could not hear the words clearly. It surprised her that the strange men spoke words Pharoah could understand.

"What are they saying out there?" Xenia asked.

"I cannot tell," Isa said.

"I pray they are here to become friends and trade," Egyptus said. "I am tired of fighting all those who travel past Egypt."

The sun moved two spans in the blue sky. Egyptus stood with Xenia and Isa, waiting for their men.

Chayim softly called down to the women, "They return."

Egyptus sucked in a deep breath and held it. The men strode through the gate, alone. Egyptus exhaled and heard both Xenia and Isa do the same. Both Egyptus and Isa placed their arms around Xenia once more.

Xenia tried to pull away from Egyptus and Isa, but they held her back.

"The men need to speak together first," Egyptus said. "They will come to us when they are ready."

Xenia swayed back and forth, readying herself to run to Pharoah's arms.

The men gathered a distance from the stairs and spoke in whispers. Egyptus strained to hear their words but could not. She, too, wanted to join them.

Pharoah and Moren broke away from the group of men and hurried to join the three women.

"What did they want?" Xenia asked.

"Food and seeds," Pharoah said. "They say they have traveled a long distance and need food and seeds to grow their own."

"And did they say they would offer something in trade for our food?" Isa asked. "We do not have enough food for every hungry army that marches past."

"They offered their service. They have little to trade yet. These people have claimed a land to the south of us. It is full of antelope, gazelles, and other animals with beautiful skins. They say they will bring skins to us in exchange for grains."

"What makes you think they will return with the skins?" Isa asked, echoing Egyptus's thoughts.

"We do not." Pharoah turned as if to stare through the wall at the group of men waiting outside. "They brought many more men with them than I would expect if they only came to carry grain. I struggle to trust them."

"May we go to the walkway to look at them?" Egyptus asked. "I struggle to know their thoughts without seeing their faces."

"Can you look out on them without being seen?" Pharoah asked. "I told them our women have all gone away."

"Away?" Xenia asked. "What would we be doing 'away'?"

"What would make you say this?" Egyptus asked.

"It felt wrong when they asked about our women. Would you be gathering eggs from the wild birds? That is what I told the leader, Jashar."

"Who is this Jashar?" Egyptus asked, walking toward the stairs.

"The leader of the strangers. He claims to be a grandson of Ham. I did not recognize him."

"Our family has changed since we left them behind on the plains of Shinar," Egyptus said, stepping softly on the stairs. Pharoah and Moren joined her.

"Remember. Do not show yourself," Pharoah reminded her as they reached the top.

Egyptus crouched low and duck walked to the wall. She rose only high enough to see.

Men stood in a tight knot. "What do you think, Animim?" Egyptus said softly, fearing her voice would carry to the men outside the wall.

"I know they say they are here to trade. But I do not trust them," Animim said.

"What did you see from the top of the wall, Moren?" she asked.

"Although we only see fifteen men standing there, I saw men trying to hide in the canals in the valley. I believe there are another twenty or thirty men out there waiting."

"Waiting for what?" Egyptus asked.

"I do not know for sure," Moren said.

"I do not trust them either," Lim said from his post not far away. "I have watched them almost from the time they arrived. Moren and Isa hurried from their home when Jason blew the horn. He did not see, but I did."

"What did you see?" Pharoah asked.

Egyptus and the others turned to stare at the young man.

"They left men and weapons hiding out there. Some are in our canals, others in our fields. They all have weapons."

"Jashar says they brought weapons to protect themselves from the wild animals. The animals and any grain they get from us," Pharoah said.

"Or to come take more, once they see where we keep it," Chayim added. "I do not trust them."

"You would not," Isa said. "The first strangers who came through hurt you. You are extra cautious."

"With reason. Perhaps they do not trust us to be honorable. I would like to trust them," Egyptus said. "But like Lim and Chayim, I struggle to do that. We should pray and ask Jehovah for assistance."

"We can do that," Pharoah agreed. "Pass this word on around the walkway. We are going to pray. Every third man should continue to stand guard against the men out there. The rest may join us."

Soon men knelt on the walkway, ready to join in Pharoah's prayer. Egyptus joined the women who knelt on the ground. They all lifted their arms.

Pharoah spoke words of gratitude to Jehovah, repeated softly by all who knelt along the walkway and on the ground. Then he spoke of their concerns that the men who were outside their walls may not be trustworthy. He asked to receive the right answer. Should they allow the men in to trade with them, or keep them out of their village?"

After a soft amen filled the air, Egyptus felt a stirring of warmth in her heart.

"I think I know what we should do," she murmured. "And I expect I am not the only one."

She nodded as Pharoah sat back on his knees, thinking. The men around them slowly stood, lifting swords and bows to the ready, prepared to fight if those outside had moved forward during their prayer.

Egyptus quietly climbed the stairs once more to peek over the wall. The men outside continued to stand in a loose group around their leader, who stood taller than the rest of the men. She sat back on the walkway, waiting for words from Pharoah.

"How full are our storage houses?" he asked Egyptus and Xenia, who had followed Egyptus up the stairs.

Egyptus considered the baskets of grain in the storage houses.

"We have enough grain to plant again and enough to last us until the next harvest, and some extra," Xenia said.

"Perhaps enough extra we can *trade* it with these men," Egyptus added. "But we should expect something in return today, not just a promise of an exchange."

"I agree," Pharoah said. "I will go speak with Jashar to see if he has anything they can trade for our food. We do not know if the rains will come or if it will flood again. We cannot give away any of our food without something in return that will be helpful to all in Egypt." He turned to Jason. "Be watchful, We will go speak with these men once more. Watch for treachery. I still do not trust them. Pass this on."

Jason nodded and hurried down the walkway, passing along Pharoah's orders.

Animim and Akish hurried down the steps behind Pharoah. Akish stopped to kiss Hulda before hurrying after Pharoah. The gate keepers opened the gate wide enough for the three men to slip through before closing it tight again.

Egyptus peeked over the wall and watched Pharoah stride toward the group of men. Animim and Akish stopped, allowing Pharoah to continue a few steps on his own. Jashar stepped away from his men to meet Pharoah in the center.

Egyptus heard Xenia hiss as she watched the men, but she kept her head low and her eyes on the men on the ground outside the wall.

"Do not attack. Do not attack," Xenia repeated over and over in a whisper.

Egyptus agreed with the thought, but stayed silent as she watched the men. Pharoah raised his arms. Jashar's arms waved around.

The men on the walkway lifted their bows and pulled back the strings, prepared to let the arrows fly if anyone attacked Pharoah. Some aimed out at the hidden men in the canals and fields.

Voices lifted. Egyptus could only hear snatches of the words. "Trade. Skins. Grains."

She prayed silently that these men would be honorable. Life would be happier if they did not always have to guard against enemies.

No. That is not true. Even if these men trade skins with us, we cannot trust them not to return or steal more from us. Nor can we expect all men to be honest and willing to trade rather than wanting to take what they want.

May we have peace, I pray, even for a year.

The foreign men trotted out of the fields. None carried visible weapons, or none that Egyptus could see. Instead, they carried stacks of skins.

Why did Jashar not say he had skins to trade? They all probably wear their belt knives and other knives hidden on them. We will have to be extra careful.

Pharoah nodded and turned back to the gate. Animim and Akish did not turn until Pharoah had passed them. Then they walked backward for a distance before turning to stride behind Pharoah through the gate.

The gate keepers allowed their men past the gate before slamming it shut and locking it. Egyptus clattered down the stairs to see what Pharoah had learned.

"I see they have skins," Xenia said before Egyptus could speak.

"They do and they will trade them with us," Pharoah said. "They wanted five baskets of grain for each skin. I told them we could get our own skins and keep all the grain for ourselves. After they agreed, I told them we would need time to gather our grain."

"What did you agree to?" Egyptus asked.

"One basket of rye or one basket of wheat for five skins."

"No oats, no barley?" Animim asked.

"No. We grow more rye and wheat during our second harvest before the rain. We have enough of these to share some, but not enough oats or barley."

"How many skins do they say they have?" Animim asked.

"Sixty this time. They say they will bring more later."

"Why do they not plant their own fields?" Egyptus asked.

"They say they have no seed. And their men prefer to wander and hunt animals," Pharoah answered. "But their women will tire of this soon."

"If they have women," Xenia murmured.

"He says they have women. I asked Jashar about his woman," Pharoah said. "He said the women wait safely on their own land."

"He said they had nothing to trade," Isa said. "I do not trust him."

"I hope no one attacks their women while their men are here," Xenia said, rocking back and forth on her feet.

"There were many women in Shinar," Egyptus said. "Where did they all go? Most were as wild and wicked as the men. Certainly they have gathered together with men."

"Or they struck off to live alone," Chayim suggested.

"No. Women know they need men to protect them and to give them children," Isa said. "Those men will have women hiding somewhere in a camp. If they steal our women, it will be to enslave us."

"I am no slave," Xenia growled, folding her arms.

Pharoah slid an arm around her waist and gave her a brief hug. "No, my love. You are no slave."

Xenia brightened and leaned close to her husband.

"How will you protect us from them if they are treacherous?" Chayim asked.

"We will have our young men carry the baskets of grain out of the village to these men of Jashar. Our older men will stand guard on the walkway with bows ready."

"And our women?" Egyptus asked, glancing around at the women waiting for instructions.

"You are our secret weapon. Jashar does not know our women are here inside the village walls. They believe they can capture you on their way back to their camp."

"Bah," Isa said. "Has he seen our women fight? Even if we were gathering eggs and feathers, we would not be without protection."

"You know that. I know that," Pharoah said. "Jashar does not know how we protect our women, or how our women fight to protect us."

"Good," Egyptus said. "Where do you want us to be?"

Pharoah laid out his plans and left to give the men their instructions.

Egyptus hurried to the knot of women and shared the instructions with them. Pharoah had a good plan.

Egyptus watched with the other women from their hiding place behind the steps leading to the walkway near the front gate as the young men and boys carried baskets of rye and wheat to the gate. Other women hid beneath the walkways around the village, not trusting the strangers.

"I did not agree to give away all my baskets," Egyptus murmured.

"How else will they carry all that grain?" Alma whispered back.

"I do not know, but I will not give away baskets again. They should have brought their own baskets. Any who want to trade with us should have to bring their own baskets to carry away their grain."

"I agree with that," Alma said softly. "I hope they carry this grain away with no treachery. Timor fears a trap."

"As does Chayim," Cira said from a short distance away.

"That is why Pharoah has us hiding here, ready to fight if Jashar's men try anything," Xenia whispered.

"Where are these men from? What did they name their new country?" Elsa asked softly.

"How did they learn to speak our language?" Hulda asked, her voice a bit louder.

"Hush! We must be quiet so those men do not know we are here," Egyptus whispered. "We will find the answers to these questions later."

Gate keepers opened the gate only wide enough for two boys, carrying a basket between them. According to the plan, after the first boys carried out a basket of rye, Pharoah stood there to accept the skins given to him by Jashar.

The four boys returned through the gate, loaded down with the five zebra skins.

Two more boys slipped past the gate with their basket of grain. They returned with antelope skins.

"I did not expect this to go so well," Elsa whispered, shifting in the heat.

"It is not over," Egyptus said, raising a hand for quiet. "We still have two more baskets of rye and one of wheat to give them. Jashar's men could still cause problems."

Boys slipped through the gate, returning with animal skins again. Egyptus felt pressure build up inside her each time two boys left, which released only a bit as they returned.

As the last two boys stepped out the gate, a shout echoed from the back wall. "Treachery! They come over the wall!"

The women stepped into their assigned fighting positions while men raced along the walkway to their positions, shouting as they ran. Many stopped along the way, as Jashar's men threw ropes up over every wall.

Pharaoh, Akish, and Animim rushed to the gate behind the boys, slipping inside ahead of swarming men. An arrow buried itself in the ground inside the village as the gate keepers banged it closed and slammed the bar down to lock the enemy out.

"Stinking, rotten, lying, soulless, cheating, sons of whores!" Animim cursed as he raced past the women and up the stairs to join the battle.

Egyptus laughed at Animim's outburst, but prepared herself with her staff to fight. She did not enjoy fighting, but would if the enemy attacked her and her family. And this enemy had taken their food before attacking.

They do not know what a nest of hornets they have stirred up.

Shouts above warned her that the men were climbing over the walls. Although the men pushed as many ropes as they could off the top of the wall and dropped rocks on their heads, the enemy still climbed up and over the wall.

Glancing around at the other women surrounding here, Egyptus waited for a man to jump or fall off the walkway. "Be ready."

She gripped her staff, then loosened her grasp and rocked on her feet.

They had discovered earlier that they had built the walkway narrow enough that the Egyptian men had enough room to fight, but those who climbed over the wall from the outside often overran it and fell to the ground where women waited to attack them.

It did not take long. Two men ran off the edge of the walkway, spinning their feet and arms and yelling as they fell.

Egypt stood back, allowing them to fall to the ground. Chana nodded her way and the two of them stepped forward to attack the men with their staffs. The fall injured the enemies, but still they rose with their swords ready to fight. Even though the enemy men were taller and had longer arms, the women's staffs kept the enemies' swords far enough away.

Egypt and the other women worked together as they had practiced and brought down all the men who fell or leapt from the walkway. Stabbing and swinging her staff, she hit the men on the side of the head, in the body, and across their legs.

Soon all the men were on the ground, unconscious. Egypt grabbed the ropes stored under the stairs and tied their hands and feet together. No more fought on the walkways, and none tried to climb up.

Between them, the five women had defended themselves against fifteen men. One or two had not survived their fall. Still, Egypt advised that they tie them. After the last attack, she did not trust they were dead.

The Egyptians took another ten men prisoners. Pharoah set guards around them.

Fearing sorcery, Egypt bent to check the ties on a prisoner. He pulled his arms from beneath him and grabbed her. A knife appeared in his hand. It scratched her throat before she could step back or pull her own knife.

He muttered something. Although she could not understand, she understood his meaning and stood quietly.

What did Arvad teach us about this? My knife ...

Her captor backed up, holding her close to him. He smelled of sweat and dead animals. Egyptus fought against gagging. He pulled her backward. She stumbled over a prisoner's foot.

Egyptus's captor screamed something. Her ear rang from it. The knife moved away from her for a particle of a breath, then set it back next to her throat.

An aching burn. A trickle down her neck. He had nicked her. She inhaled but refused to squeal or scream. Pharoah would help her escape. *My knife!* She wiggled her hands, trying to reach her belt knife, but he held her tight. She could not get to it.

Whatever else was happening, Egyptus could not tell. She focused only on the knife next to her throat.

Pharoah suddenly shouted at them for silence. "I must hear what he says."

They must be loud.

The man pulled her backward until they reached the village gate. He screamed something at the gate keepers. They refused to open the gate.

Please do not open the gate. If he gets me outside, he could take me anywhere. What will I do?

Egyptus glanced wildly around, but held her head still, fearing he would cut her more.

Prisoner

E gyptus swallowed the fear threatening to overwhelm her as the strange man dragged her toward the gate.

Her captor threatened her again. The knife edged closer to her throat. Blood still dripped from the last time the blade had nicked her. She flinched away. He laughed and said something she could not understand.

Buttercup hissed from the wall and leapt onto the man's back. Holding tightly to Egyptus, he twisted and threw himself and Egyptus backward into the wall until he knocked the cat off. Pain jolted through her.

Before she could respond, he reached down to jerk Egyptus's belt knife from her waist. She tried to kick back into him. His arm clamped around her once more. He squeezed her tight. Her hands tingled.

"Serpent," she hissed.

"Let him past gate. He kill," a voice shouted from outside the wall.

"He cannot take our woman," Pharoah called. He stood as close as he dared to them.

Egyptus stared at him, praying he could read her desire for him to free her. Her heart pounded in her head.

The man holding her shouted again.

"He kill her. You not let him out gate, now!" the man outside shouted.

Pharoah stared at Egyptus, then at the man holding her captive.

"Please forgive me. If I try to stop him now, he will kill you. I cannot let that happen, Mama. Perhaps you can free yourself from him. I will try to free you."

Pharoah was correct. She did not want him to be right. "Let us out," Egyptus said, weariness filling her soul.

Arvad, one of the gate keepers stared at her, not wanting to allow her away from the safety of Egypt and its gates.

"Let us out, now," she said. "You will find a way to free me."

Arvad nodded. He opened the gate only wide enough for Egyptus's captor to drag her through. The gate banged closed behind her.

The jarring sound of the locking bar clanging down inside sent a thread of fear through her. Jehovah had always blessed her. He would again now. If she was to die, she would go happily to join Afra. If not, she would escape this man on her own. Or someone from Egypt would free her.

The enemy leader, Jashar, shouted at the man holding Egypts in words she could not comprehend. Strange that he could speak more than one language. How had he learned these languages?

Jashar stepped close to the man holding Egyptus and spoke in a low, dangerous tone.

The man snarled an answer.

Another man rushed to Jashar with a length of rope. "Put hands in front," Jashar ordered. "Bapoto will not move knife from throat until tied."

She held her hands out and allowed the man to tie them. "Not so tight. It hurts," she complained.

With a grunt, Jashar gave another order and the man loosened her binding, though not enough to pull her hands free. She sighed as the man named Bapoto finally removed his knife from her throat.

Jashar had not learned all her language, but he had learned enough to pretend to trade. They would not get their skins back. Egyptus hoped the men from Egypt would rescue her and take back their baskets of grain.

"Go," Jashar ordered, pointing away from Egypt. "Trade for men."

"They will not trade me for all your men. I have no value to them," Egyptus argued. "I am a lowly woman."

"Lowly?" Jashar slowly circled her. "Not lowly. Well loved."

"Not," Egyptus argued.

"Enough!" Jashar's harsh words stopped her argument. "Will trade you."

He yanked on her binding rope and dragged her away from Egypt. She tripped and struggled to avoid falling. Jashar cursed at her and pulled on the rope as she steadied. Bapoto jabbered at Jashar as he pulled Egyptus past the fields and into the wilderness to the south. She watched for a way to escape, but nothing presented itself.

Long after she could no longer see the walls surrounding Egypt, Jashar stopped. His men tied her to a tall spike of granite, moving her hands to her back before knotting the rope.

"Water?" she called as they walked away. "I need water."

The men laughed. Some came close, leering at her and making rude gestures. When Jashar shouted at them, and drove them away, two stayed with swords drawn as guards.

What do they want?

She shuddered.

Fear built in her again, stronger than ever. Her body quivered and her stomach felt rock hard. While they moved, she had hoped to find an escape. How could she escape when tied to a rock?

A young man came close, but one of the older guards cursed at him.

"Water?" Egyptus begged.

The young man dropped his eyes and turned away.

Does this man mean me harm, or does he want to help?

Leering men circled her, moving their hips in vulgar ways, suggesting their desire for a woman.

'Take me home before allowing that to happen to me,' Egyptus begged Jehovah.

Jashar came toward the men, shouting and cursing at them. He carried a drinking gourd with him. The men shrugged and turned away, glancing back toward her with disgusting smirks and sniggers.

Egyptus felt like ants were crawling across her skin, biting every tiny part of her. She shuddered.

"You more than slave," Jashar said, lifting the drinking gourd to her lips.

Egyptus drank some of the water he poured into her mouth, but it flowed too fast. She choked and pulled away. Water poured down the front of her dress.

Jashar's laugh filled her with fear. She must escape this camp of the enemy.

"You more than slave," Jashar repeated. "I heard men shout. You mean something them."

"I am a woman of Egypt. That is all."

"Egypt?" Jashar lifted his eyebrows. "What Egypt?"

"Our land. We named this land Egypt."

"And where find name — Egyptus?"

Egyptus blanched and swallowed her rising fear. This man, Jashar, recognized her. None of the men inside her village had called out her name.

"What is that?" She held her gaze on him, unwilling to allow him to see her dread.

"You. You Egyptus. I heard that name."

"Not me. Where would you hear a name like Egyptus?" She wanted to cast her eyes in a circle, seeking any of her sons in the distance who would come to release her from this horror. Instead, she stared into Jashar's eyes, seeing black pits filled with hatred.

"You old. Told old woman Egyptus. Leader of village."

"Pharoah is our leader. There are other older women in Egypt. That is not me."

"Then take to Chanan. Use you. Men not have woman many ..." his eyes rolled upward as he thought. " ... suns. Men need woman."

"Not. Me." Egyptus stared at him. "I. Kill. Men."

Jashar's eyebrows lifted higher this time. "You kill men? With hands tied?"

"Wait. You will see."

Jashar left Egyptus alone, tied to the rock in the sun. Blazing heat dried her mouth and burned her skin. No other men came close to her. No one offered her water. The rough rope wore at her hands, but still she rubbed them against the rock when no one watched.

The two older, lecherous looking men stood with swords drawn, guarding her. If more than two men came from Egypt to rescue her, they could easily overtake these two men who spent more time slyly directing lewd stares at her than watching around for her sons to come to her rescue.

"Our women could rescue me from you two," Egyptus muttered under her breath.

Jashar had taken five men with him and returned to Egypt. Egyptus suspected they thought they could trade her for his captured men. There were many more men in camp than she expected after the ones they took captive. Some had died too. Where had all these men come from?

Pharoah knew it would not be wise to give the captured men back to Jashar. They would return whenever they wanted food and they would try to take a woman again. It would not work that way ever again.

Egyptus's hands smarted and tingled from rubbing the ropes against the rocks. Between the stinging roughness of the rope and the abrasiveness of the rock, she felt blood drip from her hands and wrists. She could not help it. If she was to be rescued, she would have to do it herself.

Gritting her teeth, she continued to rub the fibers of the rope against the sharp rock. It would loosen or break sometime. She hoped that would be soon, before Jashar returned angry that Pharoah refused to trade her for his men.

The young man from before came close, his face blank carrying a drinking gourd. He waved it toward Egyptus and spoke an unfamiliar word.

The older men laughed and thrust their hands toward him as if pushing him away. But the young man spoke the unfamiliar word again, adding "Jashar" to it.

Egyptus's guards came between him and her, growling at him. They would not allow the young man near her.

"Jashar," the young man repeated, along with other unknown words.

One guard growled, waving the young man forward. He took the gourd and drank from it. Water dripped from his unkempt beard. He shoved the gourd back at the young man, turning it upside down. What little water left within it dripped to the dry earth.

The young man shouted at him, using Jashar's name once more. The guards slapped their swords against their thighs, shouting loud guffaws.

The young man's face flared a brilliant red and he shouted curses at them before turning away. The guards eyed Egyptus and sneered, shaking their heads.

Her mouth had dried in the heat. Her lips had cracked. The men stood in the shade of trees, but her rocky pillar stood in the blazing sun. Egyptus wanted water now more ever.

Why were they so cruel? There was no way Pharoah would trade their prisoners for a dead mama.

She continued to scrape her hands up and down against the harshness of the rock and rope. She had to free herself, and soon.

The sun bore down on her. She stared up at it as she worked her hands against the rock, watching it move across the cloudless sky. She saw Rebecca carrying an urn filled with cool water toward her.

No Rebecca. Do not come here. They will take you.

"Go!" she said aloud. Rebecca disappeared. She dreamed. She shook her head and scraped her bindings against the rock once more.

Almost a span later, the young man returned with his water gourd. He did not speak to Egyptus's guards, who stood with their sword tips in the dirt, leaning on them. He strode between them to Egyptus.

"Voda?" he asked quietly.

She looked at him, not understanding.

He repeated the word. "Voda."

"Water?" she asked in a voice as low as his.

"Voda," he answered, and lifted the gourd to her mouth, careful to give her only a little at a time.

He repeated the word. Then added another, "Zagrozenie."

She crunched her eyebrows together. "Za-gro-zen-ee?"

The young man nodded vigorously and brought the water to her lips. "Zagrozenie."

She nodded, still not knowing what the young man said. When she finished drinking, he waved at the two men and repeated the word derisively, "Zagrozenie." Then he waved at the sun and repeated the word.

"Hot?" She tried to wipe sweat from her face with her shoulder.

He shook his head. "Ne." He grabbed his head and shook it, holding his eyes wide. Then he turned and ran in place.

"Danger?" she asked, putting a fierce look on her face.

His head bounced up and down. "Tak. Zagrozenie."

"Yes. These men think they are a danger to me."

The guard who drank all the water before shouted unintelligible words, obviously curses at the young man.

"Milosz," he said, touching his chest. "Milosz."

"Thank you, Milosz," Egyptus said.

Her guards shouted at Milosz again, and he ran away with his drinking gourd.

Perhaps Milosz would not try to hurt her. He had been kind.

Bapoto took Milosz's place, standing near Egyptus. He reached out to touch her, then pulled his hand back. "Jashar ne," he said with a frown. He reached out once more.

Egyptus's guards shouted. "Bapoto, ne. Jashar ..."

He spoke the rest of the words so fast, Egyptus could not tell one word from the next. It made no sense to her. Bapoto turned on the nearest guard, swinging his fist into the guard's face.

The guard slammed his sword grip into Bapoto's face, knocking him to the ground. Bapoto grabbed at the guard's knees and bounced back up, lifting the man off his feet and knocking the sword from his grip.

The guard yelped as he fell. Before he could rise to his feet, Bapoto was on him, pummeling him. The two men cursed, hitting each other with their fists.

Egyptus's other guard turned to watch the fight, shouting and swinging his fists in encouragement.

Suddenly, the rope fibers separated and fell away from Egyptus's wrists. She immediately wanted to rub her chafed wrists, but other men were running to watch Bapoto and the guard fight. She could not reveal her freedom in front of them.

Bits of metal passed from them to a man who shouted and wrote something on a scrap of bark. Bapoto found a rock and bashed the guard in the head. The guard rolled away from him, blindly searching for his sword.

Egyptus glanced around. No one watched her. All eyes were on the two fighting men.

She quietly slipped around to the back of the rock.

Still no one noticed.

Bringing her hands to the front and rubbing her wrists, she raced and ducked to behind a tree and away from the camp toward the waterfall dividing the Black River from the south lands. She knew the way back to Egypt from here, but it would not be safe. She did not want to lead her captors back there.

Ducking behind trees to hide, Egyptus ran away from the sounds of the combat until she heard the voices change from cries of support for the fighters to rage.

"They know I escaped," she muttered. "Jehovah, help me," she prayed as she moved closer to the Black River.

She stared into the river, seeking the log-like shapes that warned of crocodiles. Perhaps she could lure the men into the river and the crocodiles' mouths.

She stepped heavily on the sand, making certain to leave footprints leading into the river. Then she walked up through the river a short distance, watching for crocodiles as she walked.

One swam toward her, its rough, scaly back floating near. Leaping from the river onto a rock and ducking behind a bush, she ran a distance away from the river and hid among the trees. The crocodile turned and swam away.

As she hurried along, a short distance from the riverbank, she heard men shouting as they reached the shoreline. Several splashed into the river, following the trail of her footprints. She heard them cry out, "Zagrozenie!"

"You better listen," she whispered. "Those crocodiles are dangerous."

She heard men splashing in the water, then screams.

"I told you it was zagrozenie," she muttered.

Egyptus turned and picked her way through the papyrus reeds at the edge of the Black River, moving closer to Egypt.

Men shouted, but there were fewer voices now. Even one was a problem if he found her or followed her to Egypt. She reached for the knife she kept at her waist.

No knife. The memory caused her to gasp. Bapoto had taken it before he dragged her through Egypt's gate. He would have felt a second knife and taken it as well. She needed a weapon to protect herself.

As she moved silently through the island of papyrus, she occasionally glanced up, searching for serpents that dangled from above in the papyrus branches. Being taken by a serpent would be no better than having one of those men catch her.

She saw a length of papyrus reed laying on the ground. As she bent to pick it up, a serpent swung close to her head, its mouth wide open.

She grabbed the thick, dried reed and swung upward. The serpent slithered away.

The papyrus reed was not as hard as her staff, but it would do for now. She prayed the men would not force her to use it in a fight against them.

Splashing sounded close to her. She ducked and shrunk into the papyrus island, holding still. Three men hurried up the river. She saw them glance into the island where she hid, but they rushed on past. The leader moved inland, waving to the other two, calling something about Jashar.

The men feared Jashar. Good. She waited in the papyrus island. breathing shallowly so the movement would not give her away. After a long wait and hearing no one near her, she moved to leave. Just then, she heard the three men returning, this time more slowly. They must have decided they had missed her. Too bad. She shrunk back into the thickness of the papyrus island.

The men passed her island, swinging their swords haphazardly into the bushes. One man thrust his sword into her papyrus island. She leaned farther away from them. Enough that his sword barely missed her.

She held her breath until the men reached the place in the river where she had entered it.

Other men shouted at them, calling Jashar's name. The curses rose. Even though she did not understand their language, she recognized their angry curses.

Finally, she stepped from her papyrus island and hurried down the river, staying close to the edge of the water, always watching for crocodiles.

A scream came from behind. Had her captors gone into the river again? If not, what had caused the screams?

"Thank you, Jehovah," she said, hurrying toward home.

As she moved around a bend in the river, she glanced into the river. She heard a splash and looked farther out into the river. Kashet, Eber and Jov were paddling toward her.

She waved and stood still, waiting for them.

A man shouted from behind her. She glanced over her shoulder and saw one of the men who had been a guard splashing up the riverbank toward her.

Without thinking, Egyptus dove into the water and swam toward the boat. Arrows flew over her head toward the shoreline. Swimming as fast as she could, she did not lift her head to see where they went.

As she neared the boat, Eber reached down and pulled her in. "We have you, Grandmama Egyptus. You are safe now."

She lay panting on the bottom of the boat, not daring to lift her head.

Eber and Jov turned the boat and paddled against the current, inching up the river. Enemy men on the bank shouted curses at them. Egyptus stayed on the bottom of the boat until it turned once more with the river.

"You are safe now, Grandmama Egyptus," Kashet said. "Those men will not capture you again. Did you see the crocodile coming your way before we pulled you in?"

"Crocodile?" she said, gulping.

"Yes. A big one, but the man on the shore started yelling and frightened him off."

"Thank you for saving me. From the crocodile and from those men." Egyptus finally dared to sit up in the boat. She gazed around at the river. "I cannot see them anymore. They are gone." She grinned at the boys to help dispel their stress. "Why have you not taken me for a ride on your boat before this?"

"We have been busy, Grandmama," Eber said with a laugh.

"What made you decide to take your boat up the river today?" she asked.

"Pharoah suggested we take it up a distance to see if you would escape. He sent some other men through the forest, hoping to move around them and free you. He would not free the prisoners, nor would he allow those men to keep you from us."

When they reached the little dock Kashet, Jov, and Eber had built to bring their boat onto land, they blew on a shell. Egyptian men rushed out of the gate toward the river. Jov helped Egyptus step from the boat onto the dock, where Jason stood to help her out.

Eber, Jov, and Kashet pulled the boat out of the water. Eber joined the other men encircling Egyptus to protect her while Jov and Kashet lifted the boat to their shoulders. The men surrounding her walked with their bows pointing outward until they reached Egypt's gate.

The gate swung open only enough to allow the group of men escorting Egyptus through. Jov and Kashet came last, carrying their boat with them. The gate slammed closed behind them, and the bar banged down, echoing through the village.

Isa stepped from the crowd of women, surrounding her in an embrace. "Are you well?"

"I am safe at last." Tears flooded down Egyptus's face. She sagged into Isa's arms, her body shaking with relief. "I hurt my wrists, but I am safe."

Traitor

E gyptus allowed Isa to support her as she went with Isa to have her wrists and sunburn cared for. Exhaustion had left her shaking all over with little strength to stand.

"What did you do to tear up your wrists so bad?" Isa asked.

Egyptus told her about rubbing her bound wrists against the rough granite pillar.

"I know that pillar. We have stopped there on our way to our land to rest. You have damaged your wrists. I will have to put some ointment on the injury after I finish cleaning it." Isa dropped her cloth into the bowl of warm water she had warmed and stirred herbs into before washing Egyptus's injuries. "You have some deep cuts here. I need to be certain they are clean before I bandage them."

Isa set Egyptus's hands in the water. She expected it to sting, and flinched, but the herbs cooled the stinging pain in her arms.

Isa dipped the water over her wrists. "I need to be certain to get all the dirt, rocks, and fiber out of these scrapes."

"If I had not freed myself, I would still be out there. Perhaps those men would be having their way with me."

Isa stopped dipping water and stared at Egyptus with wide eyes. "They would not!"

"They leered at me, licked their lips, and moved their hips in a disgusting manner."

"No!"

"Yes. Only one young man treated me with consideration. Milosz brought me water and taught me words in his language."

Isa lifted Egyptus's hands from the water and gently dried them. "What were the words he taught you?"

"Ne —"

"I have heard that word. It think it means no."

"It does. What do you think voda means?"

"Voda?" Isa asked, reaching for her pot of honey. "We do not want these scrapes to go bad." She scooped a dollop of honey from the jar and dropped it on Egyptus's right wrist amd smoothed it over her skin. "Does 'voda' mean water?"

"It must. Milosz brought me water and told me the word for it. He also taught me another word," Egyptus said. She rolled her lips inward, thinking. "I remember. 'Zagrozenie'."

"That is a strange word. What does it mean?" Isa scooped another dollop of honey from the jar.

"Danger. Milosz said it several times. When they were running into the river where crocodiles waited, I thought 'zagrozenie.' I did not say it loud for them to hear, but some of the other men shouted it at them. They did not listen. They deserved to wade into those crocodiles."

"And be eaten by them?"

"I do not know. I only heard them scream. It amazes me how men sound like little girls when they scream in terror."

Isa laughed. "Little girl screams."

Egyptus barked a short laugh, finally seeing the humor in the situation. "Yes, I suspect they were hurt, from all their shouts and screams."

"They deserved it."

"How did you get to the water if they tied you to a rock?" Gilit asked, stepping into Isa's workroom.

"Hello, Gilit. I did not see you outside," Egyptus said.

Who invited you to my healing?

"No, you would not have seen me, but I saw you. I heard the men complaining that one of Jashar's men took you. How did you get away?"

How does it matter, I am free. You did not help.

"Look at her wrists," Isa said, holding up the one hand she had prepared for a bandage. "She rubbed them raw, rubbing her bindings against the rock where they tied her."

"Two men fought together. The one who took me prisoner, Bapoto, and one of my guards were beating on each other in a fight. My ties finally broke apart, so I slipped away."

"Is that honorable?" Gilit asked. Her face looked pinched.

"Honorable?" Isa asked.

"Yes. How is it honorable to run away from the men who captured you?" Gilit sat on a stool in the workroom.

Isa gasped. Egyptus glanced at her and shrugged.

"Yes," Egyptus said. "I think it was honorable. They had no right to take me hostage. They attacked us. They offered to trade, then climbed over our wall to attack us. I believe they are the dishonorable ones."

Gilit grunted. "Jashar would never be that dishonorable. Certainly his men attacked without his ordering it. They received the grain they agreed on." Gilit gazed at Egyptus, careful not to look at her injured hands. "Did they not?"

"They received all the grain we agreed to. We received all but five of the animal skins they agreed to give us in return," Egyptus said.

"I suspect they wanted women, in addition to the grains and seed," Isa said. "Did you see women in their camp, Egyptus?"

"No, but they were in a temporary camp, waiting for Jashar to negotiate for their men."

"We should return all their men," Gilit said.

Isa and Egyptus stared at her in shock.

"You are back. We got the skins they promised. We are even." She pushed herself up on the stool and sat up straighter.

"Are you jesting?" Isa asked, tying off the bandage around one of Egyptus's wrists.

"No. Your prisoners got what they earned, a headache and the disrespect of the other men. We should let them go." Gilit waved her hands around.

"So they can come back and attack us again?" Egyptus asked. She stared at Gilit, incredulity flooding through her.

This woman has a problem! Does she want us to give our food and lives to an enemy?

"They will not attack again. Jashar will not allow it," Gilit declared.

"And who is Jashar to you that you know what he will do and what he will not do?" Isa asked.

Pharoah entered the workroom and stared at Gilit as she slid off the stool. "I did not expect you to be here." He turned to his mama. "Jov told me they fished you from the river and you are safe, Mama. We were almost to their camp when we heard the shell sound. How did you get free?" He took her into his arms and hugged her tightly.

Egyptus repeated the story she had told Isa, leaving out the details of the leering men. Both Pharoah and Gilit stared at her as she shared.

"However, Gilit believes we should release our captives," Egyptus said as she ended her story.

"Release?" Pharoah turned to Gilit.

Gilit stepped back a step. "Yes. Jashar would not allow them to attack you again."

"Jashar would not?" Pharoah asked.

"How do you know?" Isa asked, tying off the second bandage around Egyptus's wrist.

"Jashar is a good man," Gilit said, staring at the other three. "I knew him as a child. He and Hibah's Chanan were good friends."

"He was Cain's friend?" Egyptus asked.

"You knew Cain before he came to Egypt?" Pharoah asked.

"He was Jashar's friend. I told you that," Gilit said, holding her hands up in front of herself.

"And who is Jashar to you?" Pharoah asked once more.

"He is our son," Animim said, entering the workroom. "I did not recognize him at first. His anger has changed him. But he has always been intelligent and sneaky. I am certain he listened to some of us talk together from a hiding place to learn our language. He and Chanan. That way, he could deceive us and make us think he has good intentions."

"Animim!" Gilit cried. "Our son would not do that!"

"No?" Animim said, turning on her. "How do you think he learned to speak our language?"

"He is smart. I —"

"You what? What did you do, Gilit?" Animim asked, taking her by the shoulders.

"You were gone, working on things for this silly little village. You forced me to come here when I wanted to stay in Shinar."

"I forced you?" Animim's normally quiet voice held a growing cold fury. "You insisted we come along with Egyptus. You could not be away from Tama. I would have stayed in Shinar. And we would have suffered the same curse as the rest of our family. And all you can do is work in the dark to destroy these good people who brought us with them and have treated us as family."

Gilit flinched away from Animim. "Do not hit me," she whimpered.

"I have never hit you," Animim said through clenched teeth. "Perhaps I should have. Perhaps you would not be the lazy, insolent woman you have become."

"Lazy? Insolent? If it were not for me, our son would not know our language and could not speak with us. He would not be outside the walls of this hot, nasty, beast-infested village." Gilit put her hand over her mouth.

"It was you. This whole time, it has been you," Animim said. The anger in his voice was tangible. "You taught him our language. Did you also teach Cain?"

Gilit stepped away from the stool and flicked her eyes at the others in the small workroom. "I taught Chanan at the same time I taught Jashar to speak our language. They did very well."

Not all that well.

"You taught our enemy!" Animim said.

"They would not be our enemy if they had not attacked us," Pharoah said.

"Why did Cain —"

Gilit interrupted. "Chanan."

"His mama agrees Cain is a better name," Egyptus said. "Why did Cain look for me instead of you? Did you tell him to take me?"

Gilit stood with her arms folded across her body.

"I think we need to take this outside," Animim said. "Everyone in Egypt needs to know what my ..." his mouth twisted in a grimace. "... my wife has done."

"Her penalty will be in their hands," Pharoah agreed.

"No. I will not —" Gilit cried.

"You have no choice," Animim said, firmly taking her by the arm and dragging her toward the door. "Isa, are you finished with Egyptus?"

"For now," Isa said. "I will have to examine her wrists often and apply a salve to her sunburn. Those can wait."

"Good," Animim said. "Egyptus has a right to be part of this, since she has suffered most for Gilit's actions."

He dragged Gilit out of Isa's workroom, followed by the others.

Hulda stood outside as they tromped out. "Mama, are you —? What is wrong with Gilit?"

"Come with us," Pharoah said. "We need everyone to participate in this."

Animim pulled Gilit toward the village green, where most of Egypt's villagers milled around. Some still stood guard over the prisoners. Others stood on the walkway, watching for another attack.

"Check all their ties. Make sure they are tight," Egyptus said.

"We did when the enemy took you away," Pharoah said, but he gave the order to check all the bindings. Some of the enemy had loosened their ties, but the Egyptian men tightened them before the enemy could escape.

"Can you understand my words?" Pharoah asked each prisoner.

None responded.

"Jashar is a stupid cur," Animim said with a smile.

Three prisoners turned toward him with frowns, trying to stand.

"I thought so," Animim said. "They understand some of our language."

"I told you, Jashar is an intelligent man," Gilit growled.

"And you are a traitor," Egyptus said.

Gilit tried to turn toward Egyptus, but Animim refused to allow her to move out of his grasp.

"You think you are special, Egyptus. You and your family," Gilit said with a sneer.

"Not special. I was driven out of Shinar. You did not have to come with me. You begged to come," Egyptus said. "The women of Shinar forced me to flee."

The Egyptians not guarding the prisoners or on the walkway gathered around the two women.

"What is going on?" Hibah asked.

"Why is Gilit shouting?" Ada asked.

"We will share as soon as everyone is here," Pharoah said.

"You will do this in front of our guests?" Gilit asked.

"Guests?" Egyptus asked. "We have prisoners who attacked us. Not guests. And if they understand our words, it is because of you. You will have to live with that."

Guests? How can she consider our prisoners as guests? I feared this day would come.

Even little children gathered to hear about the offenses committed by Gilit.

"Those men attacked us today because Gilit slipped out of the village to teach our language to Jashar and Chanan, whom we know as Cain," Animim announced. "My wife," his voice broke and roughened on the word, "has done all she could to make our lives miserable even on the way from Shinar to our home here in Egypt."

"I have not," Gilit said.

"You have no words to speak here," Animim said with a growl. "You have done everything you could do to ruin our lives. You refused a copy of the Book of Commandments. I had to hide the copy Egyptus graciously gave us even after you were rude to her. I smelled the meat you cooked and fed to our dogs when we were short of meat. I know it was you."

"I saw and heard you talking to your dog and shouting at other dogs," Hulda said.

"And I saw you returning full baskets of salt," Tama said.

"And I saw you taking more squash than even my big family can possibly eat in a month," Magda said.

"And you admitted sneaking out to meet Jashar to teach him our language so he could overwhelm Egypt," Animim said.

A low growl started and rose to a crescendo as the people heard and added to each accusation.

"What makes you think you can stay in our community?" Elsa cried.

Others took up the cry. "You must go!" they chanted.

Isa nudged Egyptus. "I told you this would happen one day."

Egyptus frowned. "I know. I knew it would happen, but I did not want it to be like this."

"She caused it," Isa said. "You put it off as long as you could."

Egyptus sighed. "I saw it coming. I did not want to see it happen. Animim does not deserve this."

"What do we do about this traitor?" Pharoah asked.

"She must leave Egypt and never return," Jakob said.

"Yes!" the others shouted.

"Do you all agree?" Pharoah asked, gazing up at the men on the walkway and at the guards surrounding the prisoners. "If you do, raise your hand."

Every hand lifted into the air. Even Animim's hand waved above him, although tears washed his face . Egyptus watched them raise one by one, then joined them, elevating her own arm.

"It is unanimous," Pharoah said.

"You do not have to leave too, Animim," Egyptus said.

"I knew it. You want my man," Gilit snarled.

"I do not," Egyptus said. "Animim has not taken part in your crimes. He should not be required to be penalized with you."

Voices lifted, some supporting Animim, while others said he had known and not shared with anyone.

Animim raised his arms to draw their attention. "I may or may not be as guilty as Gilit. But she is my wife. We were married by Noah for eternity. Like Adam, I will go with her and take part in her penalty. We will get our possessions."

"Take your clothing and all you can carry," Pharoah said. "You may not take any animals or wagons."

" I will take my dog?" Gilit protested.

Animim interrupted her. "Not even your dog." He turned to Pharoah. "I did not expect to take them. It will not take us long to prepare to leave. I will ensure Gilit does nothing more to cause Egypt any more difficulty." Animim gripped Gilit by the upper arm and led her toward their home.

While Animim and Gilit gathered their possessions, Pharoah waved at their prisoners. "What do we do with these men?"

"Take them out and push them into the river," Jov said.

"There are crocodiles in there!" Angetta cried.

"Yes," Jov said. "They will not return if we give them to the crocodiles."

"Or the big cats," Kashet said.

"That would be too cruel," Lexa said.

"No crueler than what those men wanted to do to Grandmama Egyptus," Eber said.

"We can drive them out and chase them across the river," Arvad suggested. "It is their problem to get past the crocodiles."

After some discussion, the Egyptians decided they would take them down the river a distance where the prisoners would chance to fight hungry crocodiles, then drive them across the river. Egyptus had convinced them that Jehovah would not be happy if they killed their enemies, even by crocodile.

"Will we force Gilit and Animim to cross the river as well?" Egyptus asked.

"No," Pharoah said, as the couple stepped back onto the village green. "They were members of our community. We will allow them to leave on their own."

Tama, Elsa, and Kib stood with their families on the edge of the crowd. They hugged their papa, but stood stiffly refusing to acknowledge Gilit when she tried to say goodbye. Tears streamed across their faces.

Gilit's face had hardened when she and Animim joined Pharoah in the green. "We are ready. Will you drive us out with your prisoners?" Gilit asked.

"No. You may go where you please," Pharoah said. "But you must stay here while we take care of our prisoners."

"I want to leave now!" Gilit cried.

"To tell them what we plan to do?" Pharoah asked. "I think not. You two can stay with Egyptus and a few others."

The younger women took the little children back to the sanctuary where they would be safe. Egyptus retrieved her staff and stood with her fighting group. Those assigned to stand on the wall to watch for enemies climbed back to the walkway, replacing the former watch group.

"No enemy stands outside our gate," Jason called.

"None stand outside the east wall," Chayim responded.

"None stand outside the south wall," Akish replied.

"No one stands outside the west wall," Lim shouted.

"Good," Pharoah said.

The Egyptians prodded the prisoners with the blunt ends of their staffs until they rose.

"Open the gate," Pharoah called to those guarding it.

Pym and Jakob held the gate open only long enough for the small group to herd their prisoners out. Then they shut it tight behind them.

"I want out! You told me we must leave. Now you force me to stay!" Gilit shrieked, trying to follow the others out the gate.

"Only until our people return," Egyptus said.

"Quiet," Animim growled, holding her elbow to prevent her from running to the gate. "You have caused these people enough trouble." He gave her arm a little shake.

Gilit grumbled as she waited.

"Sit and wait," Egyptus said. She wanted to climb the stairs and watch with her people. She needed to see if Jashar and his men were threatening to attack.

"I will go look," Xenia said, touching Egyptus's shoulder. "I do not like being left behind any more than you."

She hurried up the stairs and peeked over the top. Then she stood tall and leaned against the wall. Xenia turned and looked down to Egyptus. "No one is out there. I cannot even see our people."

Buttercup rubbed against Egyptus's legs. She bent to pick the cat up. "Thank you for trying to save me, Buttercup. Did the mean man hurt you? Maybe we will reach a time we will never need to fight off an enemy again."

They waited almost a span before Pharoah and the others returned.

Xenia raced down the stairs and threw her arms around him.

"I am safe," he said, gently removing her arms.

"What happened?" Xenia asked.

"Jashar followed us back. Most of his men followed our prisoners across the river. Only he and three of his men remain on this side. He said he would wait for his mama and papa."

"Good," Gilit said. "I am ready. Let me out of this village." She lifted her bags and marched toward the gate.

Pharoah nodded to Jakob who opened the gate wide enough for Animim and Gilit to leave.

Gilit walked past Jakob with a raised head and stiff back. Animim slumped, stopping only long enough to turn and wave sadly.

Soon the gate closed, and the locking bar fell into place with a bang.

"They are gone," Egyptus said to Isa. Her body lost its strength. "I did not expect it to happen so suddenly."

"They are gone. We will have a better life now," Isa said. "But first, I will have to care for that sunburn and your hands."

"Maybe they will teach others our language so we can honestly trade more often."

Pharoah and Xenia moved to stand with Egyptus. Pharoah put his arm around Egyptus's waist. "That would help us have a safer home."

"Hopefully, someday we will be safe," Egyptus said. "Someday."

Acknowledgments

I have worked hard to prepare this book for you. It surprises me when I form a story inside my mind and transfer it to the screen. The process is amazing. I thank you, my reader, for staying with me as I tell these stories. Without you, these would just be marks on the page.

I thank my patient husband, Jack, for his support. He waits for me to have time to give him each day and answers my questions. His support keeps my fingers moving on the keys and new books coming to you.

I appreciate the help and support that comes from my children and my parents. At 95, dad is still my final proofreader. Without the support of my family, writing would be much more difficult.

I give thanks to my new editor, Julia Allen. She has patiently worked through the mistakes and challenges of my "Covid brain," making this book and others ready for you to read. Dar Albert continues to create beautiful covers. You see her work first. I give both these ladies my gratitude.

Along with these, I thank my AngelCAST team who read the final version and found the typos and other mistakes my tired eyes and my computer program missed. Thank you, team!

I would love to hear how you liked this book. You can send me an email Angelique@AngeliqueCongerAuthor.com

Afterword

Would you like a free book?

If you have not already agreed to receive my weekly newsletter, maybe now would be a great time to join. There will soon be another free book for these readers. Or, you can read the short story about Shamgar, the healer who helped Ziva and Crites in Lost children of the Prophet. Click here to receive Damaged Healer.

If you would like a short story about Eve helping Adam, click here to receive Avenging Angel.

If you already recieve my weekly newsletter, thank you! If you have not read the free short stories, drop me an email at Angelique@AngeliqueC ongerAuthor.com and I will be happy to forward the link to either book.

Happy Reading,

Angelique

Also By

Wondering what to read next?

Find them on my Amazon Author page.

Have you read the books in the Ancient Matriarchs series? (6 books)

And the books in Lost Children of the Prophet? (12 books)

Have you found the Struggle for Limhah books? (3 books)

Did you read all the Into Egypt books? (3 books)

Look for the next series:

Abrahamic Wives

(planned to publish Summer 2023)

About the Author

Angelique Conger discovered the wonders of writing books later in her life. Books, however, have always been important to her. As a little girl in a small town, she was given her own library card at the tender age of five, highly unusual in those days.

Angelique reads a book, or three at once, much of the time. She reads most genres of books and until a few years ago only toyed with writing them. Since beginning, she has spent many hours each day learning the craft of writing and editing.

Many would consider Angelique Conger's books Christian focused, and they are because they focus on early events in the Bible. She writes of a people's beliefs in Jehovah. However, though she's read in much of the Bible and searched for more about these stories, there isn't much there. Her imagination fills in the missing information, which is most of it.

Angelique lives in Southern Nevada with her husband and Siamese cat, who shows his love by sleeping next to her legs.